THE
Rimfire Riders

A 'Catsfoot' Western

JOHN ROBB

THE CHILDREN'S PRESS
LONDON AND GLASGOW

This Impression 1971

CONTENTS

CHAPTER ONE

Fury at dawn

THEY KNEW no pity.

Fear was their main weapon and it was created by their guns. Looting was their business. They were the most dangerous men ever to move across the border from Mexico into the United States.

The twenty-three of them had the discipline and fighting efficiency of a cavalry detachment.

At the first glimmer of dawn on the fifth day of August, 1872, they rode into Meditation.

The peaceful and prosperous Arizona town was about to taste their terror.

A stray dog was the first to hear the approaching thud of hooves. And to sense what was to come.

The thin, pathetic little animal had spent a bitterly cold night trying and—as usual failing to catch a rat or a jack-rabbit. Now, tongue out and panting, it sat outside Abe Solomon's general store near the south end of the main street. Anxiously, it awaited the cascade of broken pemmican biscuits which Abe tossed to it when he opened for business each morning. Of course, it was much too early. At this hour Abe, like most others in Meditation, was scarcely out of bed.

Suddenly the dog seemed to forget its hunger. It turned away from the store. Ears jutted forward, its body began to twitch as it looked fixedly along the street. But nothing unusual was visible in the half-light.

The dog was not comforted. Instead, it raised its head and gave a whimpering howl. Then, stomach to the ground, it slunk under the boardwalk in front of the store. There it stayed, concealed and trembling in the blackness.

A couple of minutes went by. Minutes in which three veteran

5

copper miners emerged from a large and battered building which bore the sign *Pat O'Toole's Luxury Rooming House—75c. A Night*.

The old-timers grouped silently against the doorway, eyes still heavy with sleep and billows of pungent smoke wafting from their corncob pipes. They blinked blearily at a murky sky in which the sun had not yet risen.

Then, almost at the same moment, something caught their attention. They moved farther on to the boardwalk to gaze south along the main street.

"Can't see nothin' yet, but it sure sounds like we've got a whole troop of cavalry comin' this way," one of them said.

"Yep, there's plenty of 'em, whoever they are."

The third miner scratched his wispy grey head with his pipe stem. He said thoughtfully: "Seems kinda strange for anybody to ride into town as early as this. I'm . . ."

He broke off because horses and men were appearing through the thin light. They were moving at an easy canter, two abreast. But one man was riding alone and well-ahead of the others.

Watching him, a miner gave a low whistle.

"I wouldn't want to tangle with that baboon," he said quietly. "He sure does look mean!"

The leading rider was a physical giant. In height and in width he was immense—even in a territory where big men were common. It was obvious that, out of the saddle, he must have topped six and a half feet. The vastness of his shoulders and chest hinted that he could take any ordinary man in a bear hug and crush him like an eggshell.

But the menace did not end there. It showed in his gross, fleshy face, too. The skin, pitted and yellowish, bore a sheen of sweat, even though the heat of the day was yet to come. And the eyes were as dark and narrow as chippings of polished ebony. A Mexican sombrero, with a shallow crown and narrow brim, was pushing back from his crinkly black head.

Awed, half-afraid, the miners switched their gaze to the rest of the horsemen. These were dwarfed by their leader. But even so, most of them were big by any ordinary standards. And each face bore the same stamp of inhuman hardness.

One of the copper miners suddenly whispered: "Have you noticed somethin' kinda strange about that bunch?"

"We've noticed plenty and we're not likin' any of it. Just what's on your mind?"

"Their guns!"

"So they're carryin' guns. Nothin' strange about that!"

"Look again then mebbe you'll see they've all got exactly the same sort of gun. The same make, the same new model! Every durned one of 'em is wearin' a Remington rimfire with the new double-action!"

"How can you tell that?"

"Didn't I work in a gun factory before I came into mining? I tell you, them Remingtons have only been in production a year or two and they're mighty hard to come by, seein' they're the only double-action guns on the market!"

The other miner, who was less familiar with firearms, asked: "So what makes a double-action so special? Come to think of it, I've never even heard of it till now."

"They're special because you don't have to thumb back the hammer before every shot. The gun cocks by trigger pressure and that makes for faster shootin'."

By now, other people were coming on to the boardwalks to gaze at the riders.

O'Toole himself emerged from his rooming house, accompanied by more of his guests.

Abe Solomon, a towel round his neck and naked to the waist, was gaping through his partly open door. Will Hambert, blacksmith and undefeated wrestling champion of the New Territories, appeared from his workshop. Buddy Lane, Meditation's saloon keeper, who liked to think of himself as a polished gentleman, posed with careful nonchalance on his veranda while wearing a vivid pink dressing-gown and smoking a cheroot from a very long holder.

Whole families were clustering outside their homes.

But the riders paid not the slightest attention to any of them. Like army troopers on parade, they stared blankly ahead while continuing their easy canter along the main street. There was something almost eerie about it. As if they had not realised that they had left the barren, dusty trail. As if they had not noticed the people and the buildings.

It was like that until they had covered half the length of the street.

Until they were level with the Meditation Hotel.

The people were proud of that hotel. Freshly-painted outside, sparkling clean and comfortable inside, it was something out of the ordinary for any frontier town. . . .

The giant who was leading the column raised his right hand. In a space of a few yards the horses were brought to a halt. For a full minute the giant remained mounted, gazing at the hotel. While he was doing so, the tip of the sun came up. The rays seemed to strike directly into the slits of his dark eyes, illuminating them with a strange evil.

Slowly, he pushed his round fedora forward. Then he swung out of the saddle. And as he stood beside his horse, his true immensity could be seen. He almost made the animal appear a puny thing.

He turned his sweating and fleshy face towards the two riders immediately behind him. He nodded and they also dismounted. They walked stiffly towards their leader, stopping when a pace behind him.

The people of Meditation were moving, too. Drifting uneasily towards the centre of the town, drawn by curiosity, made cautious by a fear which they did not yet understand. A brooding atmosphere of approaching tragedy was settling like a shroud.

Now the giant was walking towards the hotel, the two others following.

The boardwalk creaked as his great weight stepped upon it. He paused opposite the double doors, which were closed. A hand like a joint of beef slowly turned the handle. The doors did not move. They were locked on the inside.

But they did not delay him more than a few seconds.

He braced himself in a casual fashion. And he seemed to do no more than lean against the thick teak. But the result was uncanny. There was a brief and confused sound of splintering wood, breaking bolts, twisting hinges. Then the obstruction had vanished. With a final, sharp crash the doors fell inwards.

At the same time, he strode into the entrance hall of the Meditation Hotel.

It was a large, carpeted hall, with wicker chairs and potted plants set against the walls. At the far end was the reception desk, a small and grey-haired man behind it. The man was holding a feather brush in his left hand while staring alternately at the remnants of the doors and at the giant. Downright disbelief and gathering fury showed on his craggy face.

His first attempt to speak resulted in no more than a throaty gasp. His second try was much more successful.

"What in tarnation d'you think you're doin' to my hotel? That damage is goin' to cost you plenty, mister! And when you've paid up, you can get out!"

His voice showed no trace of fear. Instead, it carried a sharp rasp of authority. Despite his smallness, despite that feather brush which he continued to hold aloft, he had the bearing of a man who was well used to giving orders.

The giant was standing in the middle of the hall, legs apart, hands on his waist. He said in tones which were oddly quiet: "You own this place?"

"You're durned right I do! And I want . . ."

"My name's Janamo."

There was a short spell of utter silence. It was broken when the brush fell on to the desk.

"Janamo?" the hotel owner repeated, his own voice now quiet, too. "Y'mean you're Janamo the . . ."

"The same. Mebbe you've heard of me, uh?"

"I've heard of you, all right! Who hasn't! But . . . but I thought you were always over the border in Mexico."

"So I was. But right now I'm in Arizona, and me and my men are lookin' for some hospitality. You're goin' to provide it . . . what's your name?"

"Fost. Major Harry Fost." He gave the information as if mumbling in a nightmare.

"*Major*, uh. Well now, so you're an army man!"

"I was. Not any more."

Janamo injected a taunting inflection as he said: "And an officer, too! Say, it's quite something to see an American officer doin' a woman's work. Better pick up that brush of yours, Major!"

A flush spread under Harry Fost's tan. He had to struggle for self-control. But he gained it and answered evenly: "You're in United States territory now, Janamo."

"So what, Major?"

"So don't get ideas about terrorising this burgh, same as you've done in Mexico. We respect the law!"

"You do, uh! From what I hear, you ain't even got a marshal in Meditation!"

"We've never needed one. Not so far. But if we ever do have trouble, we can send for the marshal and deputies at Tarran Butts."

Janamo said gently: "Tarran Butts is two days' ride from here. I make that four days at least before you could get aid. And even then, it wouldn't help you none."

Harry Fost stood back from the desk, revealing a baize apron round his middle.

"It'd help plenty, Janamo! The marshal at Tarran Butts can handle most anything. He's a fast gun—real fast. He doesn't scare easily, either. I know, because he's a friend of mine."

"That ain't quite right. He *was* a friend of yours."

"What d'you mean? He still *is*! Has been for years!"

Janamo shook his head.

"Sorry, but you're way behind the times. The marshal's dead. He's been dead for near a week."

"You . . . you're certain about . . ."

"Never been more certain about anything. It happened kinda sudden."

"What . . . did he die of?"

"A Remington rimfire bullet." Janamo tapped his polished leather holster. "*I* did it, Major! I gunned him down in the middle of Tarran Butts with the whole town watchin'!"

Harry Fost raised a hand to his forehead. It was shaking.

"You're tellin' me you've murdered him! You've come north over the border and murdered a U.S. marshal!"

"Take it easy! Who said anything about murder? It was a fair fight. Like I said, plenty of people saw it. They can't deny I licked him from a level draw. Yeah, I'll admit he was plenty fast—but he still didn't worry me none! I had him before he could lift his gun more than a couple of inches. There's nothin' on two legs to outdraw me, Major!"

The Adam's apple bobbed in Harry Fost's throat.

"You sure are claimin' a lot for yourself!"

"That's right. I carry the fastest gun on earth. *The* fastest, Major! If anybody don't believe me, he's only gotta call me out!"

"What about the deputies at Tarran Butts? There's plenty of them and they . . ."

Janamo shrugged his vastly wide shoulders.

"You've got it wrong again. There *were* plenty of deputies! But my men fixed a couple of them. The rest sort of lost interest and put up their hands. So there's no law left in these parts, Major, and we're goin' to run things our way, just the same as we did back home in Mexico."

"You mean you're goin' to take over Meditation! You're goin' to plunder the town!"

Janamo gave a soft and humourless chuckle. It sounded like a gentle splashing of acid.

"But we don't want to do that! We want you all to look after us voluntary, to be generous with us! Y'see, we don't like mean folks. If anyone here tries to be mean with us, he just won't have any kinda future." Janamo paused, allowing the threat to take effect. Then he added: "We'll be takin' over this hotel of yours, for a start. How many bunks have you got in the place?"

Some of Harry Fost's anger rekindled as he said: "I have

rooms—not bunks! There're nine of 'em and none vacant! Guests in 'em all!"

"Your guests will have to move out—every durned one! I'll be takin' the best space for m'self. My men will share the rest between 'em."

"I can't do . . ."

"You've got just five minutes to have the rooms empty and ready for us. Then I'll give you another half-hour to have a meal cooked for us. You'd better see it's good because we get raw if our chow ain't right."

The insult was uttered with disinterested smoothness. And that made it worse. It had a dramatic effect on Harry Fost. Abruptly, all sign of shock left him. Its place was taken by outraged pride and harsh defiance. The loud rasp of authority came back in his voice.

"Listen Janamo—I'd sooner play servant to a nest of rats than to you and your bunch! All my life I've kept my self-respect and I'm not losin' it now! I can't stop you takin' over my hotel, but you won't get any help from me while you're about it! You'll do your own fetchin' and carryin'!"

Janamo's eyes became even darker, even narrower. That was his only visible reaction. Otherwise, his greasy and fleshy face remained blankly expressionless.

"That's big talk from a little man," he said, keeping his voice quiet. "You'd better think again, Major."

"I've done all the thinkin' that's needed!" Harry Fost's hands went behind his back. He untied his apron. He threw it on the desk. Pointing to it and glaring at Janamo, he shouted: "*You* can wear that! You can get busy with the feather brush too, seein' this hall hasn't been dusted yet! Come on! What are you waitin' for? This is your big chance to do something useful!"

There was a tense and expectant shuffling from the two men standing behind Janamo.

But not from Janamo himself.

Janamo stayed utterly still. When at last he spoke, he seemed to do so through motionless lips.

"Major . . . you got a gun?"

Harry Fost hesitated, but only for a clipped moment.

"Yes, I have a gun."

"Get it."

"Why?"

"You're goin' to need it, that's why."

Harry Fost gave a faint smile as he shook his head.

"Not a chance! I ain't goin' in for any gunplay with you! You won't trap me like that!"

"Seems like you don't understand me, Major. I'm givin' you a chance to defend y'self."

The lines in Harry Fost's craggy face were becoming deeper. A strand of lank grey hair had fallen over his forehead.

"I wouldn't have any kind of chance against you, Janamo, and you know it! I'm no professional gunslinger!"

"Cut the speech-makin' and decide what you're goin' to do. I ain't wastin' any more time with you, Major. I'm tired of your company."

It was then, while standing behind his hotel reception desk, that Harry Fost realised his end was very near. Nothing and no one could save him. It was for this that he had soldiered with bravery through dozens of Indian campaigns. For this, he had survived the horrors of the Civil War. It was only to die at the hands of a brutalised barbarian that he had struggled to make a new life for himself as a civilian in Arizona. It was unfair. It was such a waste. . . .

Suddenly he was looking unnaturally old and infinitely weary. But his eyes showed that he was not afraid.

"I'll fight," he said.

Slowly he bent down and opened a drawer under the desk. He was fumbling in it when Janamo asked: "Your gun in there?"

"Yes, it's somewhere . . . somewhere here. By the way, it isn't loaded and it hasn't been used since I was in the Army. I'll have to check it over."

"That could be true, Major, but I'm takin' no chances. Hold it by the barrel when you bring it out."

Harry Fost did just that, laying a .44 Colt Frontier on the desk. The heavy and slightly outdated weapon bore a film of dust.

Returning to the drawer, he said: "I'm gettin' the slugs." After more fumbling, he produced an old carton of ammunition and placed it beside the gun.

He was pointing the gun to his own chest as he released the cylinder gate, showing Janamo that the six chambers were empty.

Using a pen-wiper from the desk, he cleaned the cylinder. Then he blew down the inside of the long barrel.

Re-aligning the cylinder, he aimed the .44 downward. He cocked it with his thumb and squeezed the trigger. The hammer snapped efficiently down on one of the empty chambers.

"Seems all right," he murmured, taking shells out of the carton. His fingers were steady as he loaded the gun.

Then he said to Janamo: "I'm ready, I guess."

Janamo nodded. His tree-trunk arms were hanging loosely at his sides.

"Okay, Major. You've got a loaded gun in your hand. Mine's still in its holster. Don't say I'm not givin' you a chance. Y'can make your play any time you like."

Harry Fost looked thoughtfully at his .44. It was still aimed towards the desk. But he had only to raise it very slightly while snapping back the hammer and pressing the trigger . . .

No—there was a better plan. One that could work. . . .

"There's not much space behind here," he said. "I'd like to come out front."

"You do that, Major."

Harry Fost lifted a hinged flap at one side of the desk and moved through the opening. Then he half-turned right. Now he was sideways to Janamo. And his .44 was hidden from the Mexican by his body. He took two complete paces. He was half-way through the third when he made his play . . .

He swung round, pivoting on his left heel.

His thumb descended on the gun hammer.

His forefinger flexed, ready to take first pressure on the trigger.

The Colt started to whip upwards. But it only started. That was as far as Harry Fost got.

There was a streak of orange-red flame from just above Janamo's holster. And an explosion which made the ears whistle as it reverberated against the walls.

Harry Fost had not finished cocking his gun when the rimfire bullet hit him.

He had not moved the trigger.

And the muzzle of his .44 had not risen half an inch.

The cruel force of the bullet made him continue his spin. He revolved twice, at a weird speed and like a top. Then he hurtled backwards, stopping against the desk. For a few seconds he stood propped against it, legs buckling, astonishment and fury shading his face, before subsiding slowly on to the hotel carpet.

Janamo was casually replacing his Remington in its holster. He seemed to have lost interest in this victim, who was just one more of many.

And around him, the stench of burnt powder from a rimfire cartridge tainted the dawn air with evil.

CHAPTER TWO

The broken town

GOOD FORTUNE had always protected Meditation—until the coming of Janamo. It had been a place of peace in a territory tortured by violence.

Now that the crippling Civil War was over, white settlers could at last set about exploiting the vastness of Arizona. They were helped by the spread of railroads and trail routes.

The settlers arrived from the Barbary Coast of California, from the plains of the Middle West, from the great cities of the Eastern states, and from almost every country in Europe.

Hard-eyed adventurers came, travelling alone and sniffing for the scent of any fast dollar. . . .

Whole families came in covered wagons, seeking fertile land to call their own in the one territory where, they had been told, such land was to be had for the asking. . . .

Heroes and cowards, saints and villains, the wise and the foolish—all were settling in Arizona.

And they fought.

They fought each other for every known reason and using nearly every known weapon.

Sometimes they forgot their enmities and united to fight the dreaded Apaches. The skill and ferocity of those Indians in defence of their native land was already creating a terrible legend.

But no fury had touched Meditation. In that town, life had gone smoothly on, from quiet day to quiet day. For this, there were several reasons.

Mining, for instance. It had always been important to the town's prosperity. But the scores of small mines around Meditation did not produce gold or silver. They held no promise of sudden glittering riches, had no appeal for wild,

16

brawling fortune-hunters. For only copper came out of them. Copper gave a fair return for fair work. It offered a steady living—and no more. So all the miners who worked claims near Meditation were the cautious and steady kind.

The same was so of stock-rearing.

Scorching winds from the Yuma Desert meant that there was only a small amount of good grazing land. So it was impossible to breed large herds. Instead, ranchers had to concentrate on high quality cattle and moderate profits.

Even the new Southern Pacific Railroad had done nothing to disturb the peace of Meditation. Its nearest freight junctions were nearly two hundred miles to the east. Close enough to give a gentle boost to the town's trade. But too far away for Meditation to know much about the raw, dangerous life in the settlements which were springing up alongside the railroads.

But that was not all. The railroad had also removed the fear of Indians. Apache war parties had concentrated on the railroad route, knowing that to attack and damage it was one of the best ways of harrying the whites. They were seldom seen around Meditation.

It was an artificial peace which Meditation enjoyed—and a perilous one. It created a people who were, for the most part, kindly, but flabby. People who had become unused to emergencies. And who were dazed, cowed and helpless when the Mexicans rode in.

But there were a few exceptions. A handful who, like Harry Fost, had not lost their courage.

One of them was the large, good-natured young blacksmith and undefeated wrestling champion named Will Hambert. . . .

At first, Will reacted to the shooting like all the others. He did nothing. He was shocked and bewildered. For most of the morning he sat on a stool in his workshop, staring across the main street and trying to figure it all out.

But it was hard going. Will freely admitted that he was not much use when it came to thinking. And the townsfolk just as freely agreed with him. But they were all proud of Will.

For he alone had brought a special kind of fame to Meditation
—through his wrestling.

Will had been born in one of the West's many travelling cir-
cuses, the son of a wrestler. Before he was eighteen, he was a
big circus attraction, taking on any challenger for a stake of
twenty-five dollars. No one ever beat him. Few survived more
than five minutes against him. He had a natural genius for
the sport.

Although bigger and stronger than most, that did not
account for his success. Helped by his father, he had studied
and mastered almost every known throw, hold and lock. And,
although slowish at all other times, he was lightning fast in the
ring.

The circus had arrived on its annual visit to Meditation when
Will's father died. Hearing that a blacksmith's shop was for sale,
Will decided to buy it and settle in the town. That had been
four years ago.

But Will did not give up wrestling. Several times he travelled
to big cities such as Tucson, Phoenix and Santa Fé for contests
which drew big crowds and earned him a lot of money.

In his way, young Will was famous. And people who had
never before even heard of Meditation, knew of it now because of
him. Not that this affected Will at all. He remained modest,
good-natured, and just a little simple.

It was nearly midday when he had to face the unexpected and
hideous challenge.

He was still on his stool at the open front of the smithy, when
the sound of horses cut across his thoughts.

A string of unsaddled animals were approaching from the
direction of the hotel. They were led by a Mexican walking at
the side of the front horse and holding its head by a rope halter.

Five other Mexicans, also on foot, were following. Among
them was the towering mass of Janamo.

Animals and Mexicans stopped outside the workshop.

Will thought: "They'll be wantin' them horses shoed . . . I'll
do it for 'em . . . have to do it . . . I don't want to get m'self
killed. . . ."

Janamo was moving towards Will. In the dry heat, his face was sweating more than ever and he was dabbing his chin with his neckcloth. He halted when only a few inches from the stool. Looking over the top of Will's corn-coloured head, he said quietly: "Fix new shoes on all these. And there's a stirrup chain needin' a new link. Have it all done by sundown."

Will looked cautious and uncomfortable. But his tones were civil as he asked: "How many new shoes'll be wanted?"

"A full set for all six horses."

Will shook his head.

"Sorry. Can't do all that work by sundown. It just ain't possible."

"That so?" Janamo looked at the name board outside the smithy and added: "So you're Will Hambert, uh. Well Mister Hambert, I ain't goin' back on my word. Like I said, you've got till sundown. That's around eight hours, and I reckon it's plenty."

Will scratched his head, puzzled that Janamo had not seen an obvious fact.

"No, it won't be nothin' like eight hours' *workin'* time till sundown," he said patiently. "No blacksmith works over his forge in this part of the day. Leastways, not in this territory. It's too hot. It'd near melt a man alive. I won't be able to start for another three hours, so I just can't have it done till late to-night, or mebbe to-morrow."

"Some speech you've made," Janamo said, placing his legs slightly apart and still staring over the top of Will. "You've made me feel real sorry for you! But I'm goin' to have to harden m'heart. I'm tellin' you to get busy right now, so it can be done like I told you."

Will, his guileless face tilted back, was looking up at Janamo in genuine astonishment.

"Seems like you still don't understand," he began. "Y'see it's too . . ."

"I know—too hot to sweat over your forge! But those horses need shoein' urgent." He was keeping his voice low. But every word was being produced carefully and distinctly, so they could be heard by the crowd which was gathering. It was a frightened, yet expectant crowd. Many of them were remembering that, although Janamo might be the fastest gun alive, Will was a champion fighter with his bare hands. Janamo continued: " So I'm tellin' you to start work *now*! "

" You don't know what you're sayin'! I . . ."

" Get off that stool! I'm goin' to see you over y'forge before I go. And I'm leavin' a couple of my men right here, just to be sure you don't ease off none! "

Will made a despairing gesture, as if wondering how to explain something to a stubborn child. It was because his simple mind was fully occupied trying to seek new words that he remained seated. He scarcely heard the order to get off the stool.

Janamo's right leg flashed out. The foot curled round the bottom of one of the stool legs. In the same moment, the stool was wrenched from under Will.

Will fell backwards on to the stone floor of his workshop.

And now a sudden and dramatic change had come over him. He was no longer a slightly dull, slow-witted blacksmith. His training and instincts as a wrestler had taken charge. He landed in a sitting position. But he stayed like that for no longer than it would take a rubber ball to bounce from a hard surface. He was on his feet and facing Janamo while the upturned stool was still rolling.

As the two men stood opposite each other, Janamo's enormous size was again made plain. He towered half a head above Will, even though Will was exceptionally tall. And the animal hugeness of Janamo's body made Will's well-muscled physique seem almost fragile.

Yet in those moments it was Will who looked the more dangerous. There was a shimmer of controlled rage in his normally good-natured eyes, the skin had become tight over his cheekbones.

" You don't take many risks," Will said. " It's safe enough for you to do that kinda thing to me! "

Janamo was studying Will with a faint flicker of curiosity.

"I remember hearin' about you," he answered. "It comes back to me. I guess you're the wrestler."

"You've guessed right!"

"And what d'you mean about me not takin' many risks?"

"You carry a gun and you know plenty about how to use it. *And* you got a whole bunch of other gunfighters behind you. A yip like you doesn't risk much when he starts pushin' one unarmed man around!" Will paused, pulling in a deep breath. Then he added in a rush: "I'd sure like to meet up with you some time when you don't have a gun at your side and your friends at your back!"

Janamo shrugged. He asked softly: "D'you fancy your chances in a bare-hand fight with me?"

"I reckon I do. That kinda fightin' is my business."

"Well, I'm real glad you've spoken up that way," Janamo said slowly. "I'm goin' to give you your big chance! I'm goin' to drop my gun belt. I'm goin' to fight you *your* way, Will Hambert!"

There was a quick, high-pitched sound, like the whistle of wind in the sage. It came from the crowd. It was followed by a babble of voices as, in muttered phrases, they tried to express a chaos of emotions.

The general opinion was summed up by a delicate-looking young man in a city suit who was near the front of the crowd. This was Ralph Lucas, editor of the *Meditation Gazette*, the district's recently established weekly newspaper.

Lucas said to a rancher standing next to him: "Will might beat Janamo—but what'll happen to him afterwards?"

"There's nothing we can do about it," the rancher answered. "Not now."

Lucas looked as if he were about to push forward towards Will. But after a nervous hesitation, he remained where he was.

Janamo was unbuckling his gun belt. He handed it to one of his men. At the same time he shouted to the crowd: "Make a circle!"

Pushing, shuffling, whispering, they formed a large ring in the centre of the baked, rutted road.

By now, almost the whole town was arriving. And word had reached the rest of the Mexicans, who were emerging from the hotel.

Janamo took off his fedora and his shirt. There was a murmur from the townsfolk as they saw his torso. Partly covered by black, matted hair; shimmering under sweat; it was more like the body of a gorilla than a man.

Will, standing at the other side of the improvised ring, had also stripped to the waist. He seemed formidable enough—until compared with Janamo. But that was not worrying the people of Meditation. They knew that in unarmed combat, brute strength alone was almost useless against the skill of a professional wrestler. Few doubted that Will would fix the Mexican gunslinger without trouble. But neither did they doubt that Will would have to pay the heaviest possible price for this victory. It seemed certain that Janamo would not let any man defeat him at anything, then live to boast about it.

Faintly smiling, Janamo looked towards Will. He asked: " You ready?"

Will nodded. He looked relaxed, confident.

" Ready and waitin'."

" All right. Get ready for it, champ. . . ."

Janamo injected a sneer into the last word. Then, raising arms which were as thick as most men's legs, he moved slowly towards Will.

Will moved, too. He was bending slightly forward, his own arms partly extended.

There was an abrupt silence from the big crowd. A silence so complete, it seemed as if Meditation might be part of a world which was entirely deaf and dumb.

When they were a pace apart, the two men circled. Each was watching the other with the concentration of a hunting animal.

Then Janamo attacked. . . .

His speed was almost incredible. Something never to be expected in such a giant. There was a blur of lightning movement. It ended when Janamo's left arm was seen to be hooked round Will's neck. And the immense, clenched fist was pressing and screwing into the front of Will's throat, closing the wind-pipe, threatening to choke him.

But Janamo was not allowed to retain that hold for long. Not more than three seconds. Then Will moved smoothly into a counter. . . .

He shifted his balance very slightly, lowering his left hip and pushing his left leg forward and to the right. At the same time, the open palm of his right hand streaked up. The heel of the palm hit the nerve-centre inside Janamo's elbow.

A faint growl of shock emerged from the Mexican. Instinctively, he pulled back. But Will's foot was in the way. Janamo stumbled over it, swaying like a tree in a storm.

Will moved in, preparing to finish the job. He reached for one of Janamo's wrists. His intention was clear enough. It was to whirl the arm in a circle, jerking the Mexican off his feet.

But something went wrong.

Janamo avoided the hold. He did so by dropping to the ground, his back to the advancing Will. And, throwing up his hands, he grabbed Will below the knees and threw him up and forward.

Will flew over the top of Janamo's head, hitting the ground yards away.

There was a gasp of surprise from the crowd.

Will landed easily. He was unhurt. But as he got to his feet he wore a puzzled look.

It was dawning upon him that this Mexican was a long way from being a novice at this business. On the contrary, it seemed as if he might be very much an expert. That first, choking hold could have been mere luck. But this escape and counter-throw—there was no luck about them.

They were circling again. And a harshly painful thought was clicking through Will's mind. " He's as good as anyone I've ever fought," he was telling himself. " And he's twice as strong . . . if I let him use his strength, I'll be finished. . . ."

Now Janamo was backing away, putting plenty of space between himself and Will. Will did not try to close the gap. He had an idea of what was going to happen—and he was right.

Janamo stopped. He took a couple of slow steps towards Will. Then he broke into a run. He was in the middle of a stride and travelling fast when he threw both legs into the air. His booted feet, pressed together, were flashing towards Will's face in a drop-kick.

With Janamo's weight behind it, the kick would have finished the fight there and then—if it had landed. But Will had no trouble with this move. He stood his ground, while swaying slightly back. He gripped the legs while they were in mid-air, pulling to help them on their way and at the same time giving them a vicious twist.

The twist caused Janamo's body to go into a spin. It was spinning as it hit the ground with a thud like a steam hammer. There was a shower of dust. The crowd pressed back as he rolled towards them.

He rolled four times—very fast. Then he was on his feet, glaring at Will and using the back of a hand to wipe mixed sweat and dirt from his face.

The speed of the recovery had been astounding. It gave Will no chance to follow up. And it showed that the Mexican's sheer toughness made it almost impossible to hurt him seriously.

Janamo was again moving slowly forward. His right fist was bunched.

Will thought: "If he's goin' to try an ordinary punch, I'll be able to trap his arm and . . ."

Janamo's fist flashed forward. At the same time, the fingers opened. A handful of dust from the road hit Will full in the face. A lot of it went into his eyes.

Searing pain made Will close his eyelids. Blinded, he rubbed them frantically while backing away.

He felt something tighten round his body, just above the waist. Something like the crushing coils of a python.

Will knew that Janamo, standing behind him, was tightening his arms in a bear-hug which would surely splinter his ribs. Already the pain in his body was more intense than that in his eyes.

Will kicked backwards. But his boot met no resistance.

Janamo, knowing too much to be caught that way, had spaced his feet wide apart.

There was another possibility. Another possible escape from the bear-hug. . . .

Bending his knees, Will lifted his feet clear of the ground. Now Janamo was left supporting the whole weight of Will's body. Which meant that the pressure should relax, that he should slide to the ground and out of the Mexican's grip.

But nothing of the sort happened. Without apparent effort, Janamo held him in mid-air and continued to increase the cruel pressure.

Will felt white hot spears of agony shoot up from the region of his compressed kidneys and shatter against the inside of his skull. He felt his lower ribs bending inward. He was blinded and helpless in a world of torment.

And he heard Janamo talking to him. Janamo hissing into his ear.

"Beg for mercy, champ!" he was saying. "Beg for mercy and mebbe I'll let go!"

Will could not answer in words. He had not enough strength left to get breath to his vocal chords. But he managed a reply which was clear. He shook his head from side to side.

"Okay—if that's the way y'want it!" Janamo said. And he again tightened the circle of suffering.

Will listened to a sound like water pumps at work in his head. Working faster . . . faster . . . Then they seemed to explode. . . .

That was his last memory before passing into a merciful unconsciousness.

Janamo held Will's slack body for several seconds, smiling as he looked at it. Then he stared at the dazed, incredulous crowd. He turned slowly round, so that all could see the flopping, senseless man in his arms.

Raising his voice to a bellow, he told them: "Take a good look at him! This is your champ! This is the man who thought he could lick me in a bare-hand fight! Well, mebbe you understand now! Mebbe you've got the idea that there's no man alive who can lick Janamo, with or without guns!"

As he finished speaking, he tossed Will Hambert away from him. Will landed like a discarded sack at the edge of the crowd.

It took time for the people to recover their wits. Then three men picked up Will and carried him towards the house of the town doctor.

Laughter from the twenty-three Mexicans followed them.

Four hours later, Ralph Lucas met the challenge. The battle was fought in the office of the *Meditation Gazette*.

The weekly newspaper office was in a side-street at the north side of town. It had been a livery stable for thirty horses until Lucas took it over less than a year before. Now nearly all the space was occupied by a steam-powered flat-bed printing machine, cases of type and other necessities for producing a paper.

All the horse stalls except one had been removed. The exception now contained an untidy table, a couple of chairs, and hundreds of galley proofs suspended from hooks in the three wooden walls. This was where Lucas did his writing.

Lucas was sitting behind his desk, talking to the only other member of the *Gazette* staff.

The two made a peculiar contrast.

Lucas was thin, almost frail-looking, and the fact that he was clever showed in his sallow, young face.

Bason Thebes, his handyman-assistant, was fat, pinkly healthy, and his roly-poly face suggested, correctly, that he was a harmless fool.

Lucas was modest, painstakingly accurate in everything he wrote and said.

Bason was a boastful liar and—like most of his kind—he was stupid enough to think that people believed his fantastic stories.

" It comes to this," Lucas was saying in his cultured voice, " we either stand together against that gang of gunslingers, or we may never know any peace again. If we grovel to them, they'll go away—but only to come back whenever they feel like it."

Bason nodded vigorously. " Just what I was thinkin', Mister Lucas! We gotta get tough with them Mexies! I remember when I was a colonel in the Federal cavalry, I came across . . ."

" Tell me about it later," Lucas interrupted quietly. " Much later."

He was used to Bason's heroic stories and, being kind-hearted, often pretended to take them seriously. But he was in no mood to listen to them now. He was talking to his handyman for just one reason—he was in such a state of suppressed fury that he had to talk to someone. And Bason was the only person available.

" But this is interestin'," Bason persisted.

" Then I'll look forward to hearing it some other time."

" Y'see here I was, a colonel in the cavalry, and outside this small town I met up with a . . ."

" You said this was an interesting story?" Lucas asked bleakly.

" It sure is!"

" Well don't spoil it by trying to tell it now. Save it for when I've got time to enjoy it."

" But you're not doin' nothin' right now, Mister Lucas!"

" I will be doing plenty very soon. The next edition of the *Gazette's* going to have a lot to say about Janamo and his killers and I'm going to get right down to writing it."

Lucas cleared a space among the litter on his desk and drew a pot of ink, a pen, and a pile of fresh paper towards him.

Bason suddenly forgot his story. Anxiety creased his round face. He stood on one fat foot, then on the other.

" D'you mean you're goin' to write somethin' about them Mexies?" he asked cautiously.

" I certainly am."

" Somethin' *against* 'em?"

" There's nothing to be said for them."

" But . . . but won't that be dangerous? I mean, they're right here in town. They'll read it and . . . and they won't like it!"

Despite the far more urgent matters on his mind, Lucas was faintly amused. Dipping his pen in the ink, he said blandly: " But danger doesn't bother *you*, Bason."

Bason Thebes contrived a sickly grin.

" Oh, that's . . . that's right, sir. But y'see . . . it's not m'self I'm thinkin' about!"

" Really? Who are you thinking about?"

" You, Mister Lucas. I wouldn't want you to run into any trouble with Janamo."

Lucas lowered his head, partly to begin writing and partly to hide a fleeting smile.

" But surely I'll be all right while you're around, Bason? After all, you're a top-gun yourself. You've told me often enough. You've won scores of gunfights. You've told me that, too. So I guess I don't have anything to worry about from Janamo. Not while I've got you to protect me."

Bason's face had changed colour. It had assumed the hue of an over-ripe cheese. His hair seemed to have become stiffer, more upright, so that it was like the coat of a frightened cat. His round eyes were like protruding marbles. He began to stammer.

" Y-y-yep . . . but I . . . y'see I c-can't always be around to l-look after you, Mister Lucas. I mean, if J-Janamo's mad with you he'll m-most likely come for you while I'm not here."

Lucas was writing. Without looking up, he said: " You almost sound as if you're scared, Bason. But of course, you can't be. Not an intrepid man like you!"

" C-certainly not! Me s-s-scared of a cheap yip like that J-Janamo? I'd deal with h-him fast enough, I can tell you! It's only that . . ."

There was a creaking of a floorboard behind Bason. Janamo was standing behind him, just inside the entrance to the room. Janamo's thumbs were stuck into the front of his gun belt. His fedora was pushed far back from his head, so that it was only held in place by the chin strap. His face was as expressionless as a slab of wet concrete.

Janamo said softly: " Here's y'chance to deal with me, fatso! Y'can start right now!"

Bason rose into the air as if jerked there by an invisible wire. When he returned to earth he was a quivering mass of helpless blubber.

Lucas looked up. There was a slight shake in his hand as he laid down his pen. But his voice was firm.

" I didn't hear you come into my office. There's a place to wait just inside the front entrance."

" I can move nice and quiet when I want to," Janamo said. " And I don't wait for no man."

" So it seems. What do you want?"

" Just lookin' around."

" This is a newspaper office. You won't find anything to interest you here."

" I ain't so sure about that. I've just heard some talk between you two. It was durned interestin' to me."

" Was it? Well, I'm not going to discuss it with you, Janamo!"

The Mexican came farther into the room. He stopped opposite the desk. With a casual sweep of his hand he sent the ink pot and a great pile of papers on to the floor. Then he sat on the cleared space. And he bent towards Lucas, still towering over him.

" You're Ralph Lucas, uh? You're editor of this print sheet? That right?"

" It is, and . . ."

" I'll do the talkin'! From what I overheard just now, it seems like you're plannin' to write somethin' about me in y'paper. Somethin' that ain't nice!"

Lucas's cheeks were pale and drawn as he answered tersely: " That's right."

" Well, you'd best think again! You ain't goin' to put anything in y'paper about me that I don't like! Get it?"

" Yes, I get your meaning. But I still intend to please myself. There'll be no peace for anyone till gunslingers like you are put out of the way and I'm going to say just that!"

Janamo looked blankly at the wall behind Lucas's head as he whispered: " You're goin' to write about us, that's for sure. But not the way you say! You're goin' to put a nice friendly piece in your paper about us!"

" Am I?"

" You sure are! You're goin' to say how glad the folks of Meditation feel about havin' us here as their guests! How it's a fine experience for all of 'em. You're goin' to tell 'em how grateful they ought to be to us."

Lucas sat slowly back in his chair. He looked at Janamo with a blending of surprise and curiosity.

" You think I'm going to do that, do you?"

" If you know what's healthy, you will!"

" Just as a matter of interest—how do you think I could explain away the murder of Harry Fost? And the half-killing of Will Hambert?"

" That'll be easy. You're goin' to say how that hotel-keeper just begged for trouble and I had to shoot in self-defence. You'll tell your readers that I didn't want no trouble with him, but he fancied his chances in a gunfight with me. Just seekin' glory, I guess. And as for Will Hambert, you'll take the same line."

Lucas was breathing quickly. Two angry red spots now broke the pallor of his cheeks.

" If you think I'd write and publish lies like that, you must be crazy! I'd never be able to hold my head up in Meditation nor anywhere else again!"

Janamo opened the palm of his right hand. He rubbed it slowly against the butt of his double-action Remington rimfire.

" Mebbe you won't have no head to hold up, if you don't do like I say!"

Lucas looked at the gun. He was afraid. There was no doubt about that and he admitted it to himself. He was afraid of Janamo, afraid to die. But he also knew that he would rather be killed than obey this order. He shook his head.

" No."

Janamo's fingers closed round the gun butt. Very slowly he lifted it from the holster. Equally slowly, he raised the barrel until it was aimed at the centre of Lucas's forehead.

"You gave the wrong answer, Mister Lucas! Try again!"

Lucas got to his feet. Janamo raised the gun slightly, keeping a bead on him.

Speaking quietly, Lucas said: "Listen, Janamo, because I'm going to tell you something that's new to you. A year ago I gave up a job on a big paper in the East. I used all the money I'd saved to buy printing plant and have it freighted out here so as to start the *Gazette*. I did it partly so as to earn a living and be editor of my own paper. But that wasn't all. There was something else, just as important. I figured that new, frontier towns like this need good newspapers because the people have to know what's happening all around them before they can form proper opinions, govern themselves in a democratic way and live in freedom. Those newspapers have to give the facts. They have to be run by men who won't ever be scared to tell the truth. Men who'll never be corrupted and never be bullied. That's the sort of editor I've hoped to be. If you're going to kill me, get on with it—but I'll never tell downright lies in the *Gazette* just to save my skin. If I did that, I'd be betraying everything that good newspapers stand for!"

Janamo pursed his moist lips. He gave a soft whistle.

"That was some speech, Mister Lucas."

"It's the way I feel and nothing will change it."

Janamo took a slow pressure on the trigger. The hammer moved back, the cylinder began to turn. Lucas braced his frail body and closed his eyes.

Holding the hammer quarter-way back, Janamo watched him carefully. For a moment he seemed almost puzzled. Then he produced a deep rumbling laugh. He eased the hammer slowly forward until it was again at the safety position. Then he returned the gun to its holster.

"Okay—I won't finish you, Mister Lucas. I've thought of a better way of makin' you do like I tell you."

Lucas opened his eyes. His entire body was shaking. He looked as if he might faint as he flopped into the chair.

"Nothing will make me write to your orders," he muttered weakly. "There's nothing you can do!"

"How'd you like to lose all that printin' machinery you've got?"

"Lose it . . .?"

"Yep—have it broken up! I've got a few of my men right outside. I guess it won't take 'em long to fix things so that there's nothin' to print your paper with! You did say you'd spent all your money on the plant. It'd be a pity to lose it all, wouldn't it?"

Something akin to a sob escaped from Lucas's throat.

"The answer's still no," he whispered.

Janamo shrugged.

"If that's the way y'want it, it's the way it'll be. . . ."

He strode out of the room, ignoring a palsied Bason Thebes, who was cowering against the wall.

Lucas heard Janamo bellow to some of his men.

He heard heavy feet tramping into his front office.

He winced as a succession of crashes told him that trays of type were being cascaded on to the floor, that the flat-bed printing machine and its steam motor were being wrenched and hacked apart. . . .

But he did not see it because his eyes were closed again. And he was silently weeping.

CHAPTER THREE

Trail scout

THE MARSHAL of Tucson City tossed his hand of playing cards on to the table. He yawned, stroked his greying moustache and looked out of his office window.

"You've won seven dollars from me," he said to his senior deputy, "and that's as much as I can spare on my pay. Pour me some more coffee."

The deputy went to a kerosene stove and emptied an extra handful of brown beans into a simmering pot.

"It's kinda quiet right now," he said.

"So what? You're not complainin', are you? We can use a bit of quiet now and then in this burgh."

"No, Marshal, I'm glad of the rest, the same as you—by the way, that big wagon train from San Antio arrived a couple of hours back."

"I know."

"Didn't you say somethin' about their trail scout bein' a friend of yours?"

"Catsfoot? Yep, I've known Catsfoot quite a time. But it'll be all of three years since he was last in these parts. In his job of guiding wagon trains he travels most everywhere from the Dakotas to California. I'm expectin' him to call on me sometime this afternoon."

Pouring the thick coffee into mugs, the deputy said: "I've heard about Catsfoot of course. They do say he's some man."

The marshal nodded, sitting back and putting his feet on the table.

"Just about the best trail scout there is. When wagon trains are assemblin' to cross Injun country, they'll wait months till he's free to guide 'em. Catsfoot must've scouted for hundreds of wagon trains and I'll wager none of 'em has ever so much as sniffed a hostile Injun while he's been in charge. He never loses the way, neither. Not like a lot of other scouts do. Yep, you're right when you say he's *some* man."

The deputy put the mugs on the table and sat opposite the marshal.

"What about his guns?" he asked.

The marshal raised his eyebrows.

"His guns? What's on y'mind?"

"I've heard folks say he carries two of 'em and . . ." The deputy hesitated, looking uncomfortable.

"And what? Let me know what you've heard!"

"He's supposed to be one of the fastest guns west of the Great Plains. Uses the double-draw, too. Some folks say there ain't a gunfighter like him anywhere in . . ."

The marshal raised his heel and brought in crashing down on the table, spilling some of his coffee.

"Don't ever call Catsfoot a gunfighter again! That's an insult!"

"But I thought he . . ."

"Mebbe he *is* one of the fastest guns alive, but he don't go around boastin' about it! He don't try to make trouble, neither! Catsfoot uses them guns of his only when he has to—to defend himself or other folks. He thinks of himself as a trail scout, pure and simple, and his guns . . . well, they're just part of his equipment, I guess, and the less he has to use 'em, the happier he is."

"Sorry," the deputy said, slightly crushed. "I didn't mean no offence." He hesitated, then chanced a question. "Have *you* ever seen him use them guns of his, Marshal?"

The marshal nodded, sipping the remains of his coffee.

"Just once, and that was in Santa Fé, not long after the Civil War. There was a quarrel in the Blue Star Saloon and two men were tossed out on to the boardwalk. One of 'em starts to walk away. The other pulls a Bowie knife and throws it at this other hombre's back. Catsfoot happens to be standin' mebbe ten yards away. He saves that man's life by drawin' his guns and shootin' that knife into pieces while it was still spinnin' in the air! I saw that with m'own eyes," the marshal concluded flatly.

The deputy was silent for a time, then he said: "I sure am lookin' forward to meetin' him." Changing the subject as another thought occurred to him, he added: "There's a stage due in from Meditation this afternoon. It'll be the first for all of three weeks and that seems kinda strange to me. They usually come in every seven days."

The marshal showed no particular interest.

"Meditation. When the burgh's not half-asleep, it's only half-awake," he muttered. "Seven days . . . three weeks . . . it's all the same to them!"

The deputy, who was ambitious and conscientious, said: "I ain't so sure. As well as carryin' passengers, the stage coach is important for that newspaper they've got. It picks up regular packages of news messages from the east at the railhead and takes 'em back to Meditation to be printed. How will their newspaper get out if it don't have any news?"

The marshal was not lazy. But neither did he believe in meeting trouble half-way.

"Mebbe the editor's takin' a rest," he said.

"What about Tarran Butts, too?" he asked. "That's another place we haven't been hearing from in a long time."

For a few seconds the marshal was thoughtful. Then he answered: "Neither of them places has anything to do with us. Meditation's two hundred miles away and Tarran's nearly twice as far. Anyway, they've got a good marshal at Tarran and plenty of deputies who're able to handle any trouble that comes along. And they keep an eye on Meditation, too."

"All the same, it seems a bit strange."

The marshal was becoming impatient.

"Listen, a stage from Meditation *is* due any time now, isn't it? If anything's wrong, we'll soon hear about it when it arrives!"

"Mebbe I'd better ride out to meet it."

"Don't talk crazy! What good would that do? Wait for it in town, if you like."

The deputy moved towards the door.

" I'll do that," he said, going out.

Left alone, the marshal stared into his empty coffee mug for a long time. Reluctantly he admitted to himself that the silence from both towns was very unusual. If only they had telegraph offices, he would be able to settle the matter in a few minutes. But neither Meditation nor Tarran had got round to having that sort of modern convenience.

He was still brooding when the door opened. A man in buckskins paused on the threshold.

A man who was very tall and slender. His fair hair was worn long to his shoulders, in the fashion of many trail scouts. He carried a pair of Colt Dragoons, slung low at his hips from a single gun belt.

But it was his face which held attention. Smiling slightly now, it was a type of face seldom seen in the frontier territories. Only lightly bronzed, the features were finally modelled. His blue-grey eyes had strength and kindness in them. It might have been the face of an artist or a poet. It seemed almost out of place under a stained, wide-brimmed fedora.

" Hullo, Marshal," Catsfoot said. " Glad to be meeting you again."

The marshal jumped to his feet and they shook hands in the middle of the office.

" I knew you were in town," the marshal said, slapping Catsfoot's back and pushing him towards a chair. " But I didn't come to see you right away because I knew you'd be busy checkin' out your wagon train. Was it a good trip?"

" Middling good," Catsfoot said, sitting down. " Some Indian war parties are busy east of the Apache Mountains. I had to detour the wagons over the Pecos River to keep clear of them, but we've made out all right."

The marshal brought over mugs of fresh coffee. " You been to Santa Fé in the last couple of years, Catsfoot?"

" Only once, about six months back."

" D'you remember that time when we were both in Santa Fé and . . ."

Relaxed in the marshal's office, drinking coffee, the two friends discussed places and people they both knew. It was late in the afternoon when Catsfoot got to his feet and the marshal said: " You'll be havin' supper with me to-night, Catsfoot?"

Catsfoot smiled.

" Thanks, I'd like that."

" That's fixed, then. We seem to be havin' a quiet spell right now, so I'll be able to take time off to show you around. . . ." He hesitated, then continued more seriously: " But there's one thing on m'mind . . . you know a burgh named Meditation?"

" I know where it is, but I have never been there."

" Tarran Butts?"

" Yes, I was once in Tarran."

" Well, my senior deputy's set me thinkin' about both those burghs . . ."

The marshal told of the unusual silence. Catsfoot listened carefully.

" There could be a simple reason for it all," Catsfoot said when the marshal had finished. " You know that at least there's a stage due in from Meditation, so you'll hear . . ."

He broke off as the door was pushed open. Two men were entering and one of them was the deputy. The other was bent and crippled. He was supporting himself on crutches. His head was downcast, as if in shame, so that his face could not be clearly seen.

The crippled man hobbled painfully into the office. There was something about him which suggested that his spirit, as well as his body, might be broken.

Before anyone could speak, Catsfoot lifted a chair towards the man and helped him into it. He grunted a faint thanks and sat huddled and withered, staring at the floor.

The deputy pointed towards him and said: " He's just come off the stage from Meditation. Mebbe you don't recognise him right now, but you know him. You've seen him in the wrestlin' ring. He's Will Hambert. . . ."

That night the marshal visited the home of the governor of

Arizona Territory. It was a large and luxurious house in private grounds, three miles outside Tucson. The marshal, freshly shaven and in his best clothes, always felt uncomfortable in the place and this was no exception. The deep arm-chair in which he sat was too soft, the thick carpets and expensive furnishings too overpowering. The governor himself—a quick-talking, go-getting politician—was overpowering, too.

" Something's gotta be done, sir," he said after re-telling Will Hambert's story. " At least three lawmen have been murdered by Janamo and his gang at Tarran Butts. A hotel-keeper's been gunned down at Meditation. And both towns have been looted."

The governor wore newly fashionable pince-nez spectacles clipped to his beaky nose. He took them off and carefully polished them with a white silk handkerchief.

" It's a difficult situation," he said. " What do you suggest?"

" Well, I can't do anything, sir. I'd need most of a hundred well-trained men to be sure of rounding up a gang like that, seein' they're all top-guns and well-disciplined, too. I couldn't raise anywhere near that number. And even if I could, what about this place? I couldn't leave it without protection while we hunted the territory for Janamo. We might be away weeks, or even months."

" I agree," the governor said, replacing his pince-nez and putting the tips of his well-manicured fingers primly together. " But you still haven't answered my question. What do you suggest?"

" Guess there's only one thing for it, sir—you'll have to call in the army."

" From Fort Dexter?"

" It's the only place that's near enough, sir. They have a telegraph post at the fort, so you can get a message to the commanding officer right away."

The governor shook his head.

" That can't be done, Marshal. The garrison there is already strained to the limit protecting the railroad against Apaches."

The marshal was surprised and annoyed.

"But these are *people*, sir! I guess they're more important than a railroad!"

"You don't quite understand, Marshal. It happens there's a government order from Washington that says the railroad's to have every protection. There'd be serious trouble if I were to put the railroad in danger because I sent soldiers away to chase a bunch of robbers."

"Robbers!" The marshal could not disguise his mounting indignation. "They're not just robbers, sir! They're killers!"

The governor sighed impatiently.

"All the same, I'm not going against instructions from Washington."

"But y'can get special permission from Washington! Y'can do it by telegraph—the relay stations can have a message there by morning! When they knows what's happenin', I figure they won't mind a company of troopers being sent after Janamo!"

The governor said: "Please don't shout at me, Marshal."

"I'm—I'm sorry, sir, but . . ."

"You wouldn't understand, but other very important people are concerned as well as the government. Those people would be very, very annoyed if anything endangered the railroad."

The marshal, who was very far from being a fool, drew in a deep breath. He was simmering with fury and he decided to say what was on his mind.

"Y'mean the businessmen who own the railroad would be upset, sir! They want all the soldiers watching their property, and to blazes with towns like Meditation and Tarran Butts! Those towns don't matter and the folks in 'em don't matter to the big businessmen because they ain't makin any profit out of 'em, like they are the railroad!"

The governor said icily: "Millions of dollars have been spent building the railroad. The people who've put up the money are entitled to proper protection for their property."

"Okay, but what about the ordinary people, sir? Aren't they entitled to have their lives and property protected, too?"

The governor got abruptly to his feet, a hint that the interview was over.

" There's nothing I can do at the moment," he said. " In any case, I don't know why you're so worried. It seems that this gang left Meditation several days ago."

" But they'll be takin' over other towns, that's for sure!"

" I don't think it's at all sure, Marshal. Good night. . . ."

A further pressure of words built up in the marshal's head. He wanted to say that he knew why the governor was anxious not to annoy the railroad owners. It was because the governor had political ambitions. He hoped to stand for Congress. But these influential businessmen could soon put a stop to that, if they were displeased with him.

But he realised that to say this would be useless. It would not change the decision. And, most likely, he would be removed from his job as marshal.

The marshal was still simmering as he left the governor's house, mounted his horse, and rode back to Tucson at a hard gallop.

There was a pendulum clock in the marshal's office and it showed midnight. Catsfoot glanced at it and said: " We've been talking for a long time and all we've done is decide that the governor's no use."

He and the marshal were sitting opposite the kerosene stove.

The marshal was silent for a full minute after Catsfoot had spoken. He stared at the stove, smoothing his grey moustache. Then he said: " We haven't decided anythin' because there's just nothin' we can do."

Catsfoot got to his feet, lacing up the front of his buckskin jacket.

" I'm not so sure," he said. " It seems to me as if an outfit like Janamo's would have one weak spot."

" I can't figure what that'd be."

" I guess it'd be Janamo himself," Catsfoot said.

The marshal looked up incredulously.

" Janamo the weak spot? That's crazy! I've heard plenty about that Mexican and there ain't nothin' weak about him! He's the makin' of that mob of his. He's turned 'em into a small army. Sure, he can outdraw most anyone and he has the strength of Goliath. But that ain't all. They do say he has brains as well."

"That's just what I mean," Catsfoot said. "They all rely on him. Without Janamo, they'd be nothing."

"Mebbe so, but that don't get us any place. Janamo don't look like he's thinkin' of retirin' to any dairy farm! He aims to stay with his outfit for a long time."

Catsfoot moved silently, gracefully towards the window. He was looking through it and into the dark street as he asked: "Doesn't Janamo claim to be the fastest gun on earth?"

"That's right—and nobody's ever proved him wrong."

"But just suppose he was challenged to a gunfight . . . and suppose he was licked . . . that'd finish the whole outfit off for good, wouldn't it?"

"Listen, who'd be crazy enough to challenge Janamo? And who in tarnation would have any chance of lickin' him in the . . .?"

The marshal's voice faded. His eyes were suddenly fixed on Catsfoot. Catsfoot had taken his right-hand Colt Dragoon from its holster. He was spinning the cylinder, looking carefully along the top of the slender barrel.

"Go on," Catsfoot said, dropping the Colt back in its holster. "What else were you going to say, Marshal?"

"You?" the marshal asked very softly. "Don't say *you've* got the notion of takin' on Janamo?"

"That's what's in my mind."

The marshal sighed and shook his head.

"Listen, Catsfoot, I know what you're like with them guns of yours. I've seen you use 'em! But you've gotta face up to facts—Janamo's as fast as light, too. He *could* be faster than you, Catsfoot. They say it doesn't matter how quick you are, there's always another gun, waitin' somewhere, that's quicker!"

Catsfoot nodded. His face was serious.

"I know that, marshal. And it seems, as far as I'm concerned, the man to outdraw me might be Janamo. I'll just have to take my chance."

"But it ain't worth the risk! As often as not, when two top-guns meet they finish killin' each other, because there's not a split-second between 'em. *That* could happen! Thanks for the offer, but forget it! I'm not expectin' you to do the work of lawmen!"

"There aren't any lawmen around to do the work. Those that've tried, have all been killed. And there's no hope of calling in the army. So the man with the best chance has got to face up to Janamo—and I figure it's me."

Taut with anxiety, the marshal moved towards Catsfoot.

"Y'know what you're thinkin' of doin', don't you? You're aimin' to go around deliberately lookin' for a gunfight! That's somethin' you've never done, Catsfoot—never in all your life! Only lawmen are entitled to do it!"

Catsfoot answered: "It's true that the fights I've had have all been forced on me. And I'm not proud of any of them because I don't like gunplay and I never will. I'll be a durned happy man when men don't have to carry guns in the New territories. But just this once, I'm going in search of trouble—I'm going to bring Janamo out to face me. Don't you see, it's got to be done if peaceful folks in the territory are to know any peace!"

The marshal made a despairing gesture.

"Okay, but how d'you know you'll be able to find Janamo? It might take months to catch up with him and you can't spare that kinda time. Don't forget you've got contracts to guide wagon trains."

"I'm sending a message cancelling the next contract. As for Janamo, I'm not going to try to catch him."

"But how . . .?"

"I'm going to let Janamo come to me. I'm going to Meditation. When I get there, I'll spread word that I'm waitin' for that Mexican. That sort of news spreads fast. He'll hear about it soon enough. And a man like that won't be able to resist coming back to Meditation just for the pleasure of trying to gun me down. Gunslingers like him can't stop—they have to go on proving they're the fastest."

The marshal sighed. He made a last effort.

"Mebbe you've forgotten somethin'—even if you do lick Janamo, you'd still most likely be killed! There'd be all his men with him and they'd never let you get away with nailin' their boss!"

Catsfoot took his fedora from a wall hook. Pushing back his long, fair hair, he put it on his head and tightened the chin strap.

"You could be right," he said.

"Then—then don't you care about your own life? D'you *want* to throw it away? This is crazy!"

"Of course I don't want to throw my life away," Catsfoot said, his calm blue-grey eyes meeting the marshal's. "But when people are in danger and just one man might be able to save them, then that man's got to try. If he doesn't, I guess he's no man at all."

"But your life's valuable to a whole lot of people! The wagon train rely . . ."

"I guess the lives of the lawmen at Tarran Butts were valuable, too. That didn't stop them trying. Same with that hotel-keeper in Meditation—and from what I hear, he never had any kind of chance."

The marshal watched as Catsfoot took a pair of deerskin gauntlets from his jacket and pulled them on.

"So you're leavin' right now?" he asked.

"There's no time to waste."

"But you only got in with the wagon train this afternoon. You must be weary. You need to sleep awhile."

Catsfoot smiled and shook his head.

"I'm not tired yet. When I am, I'll rest on the trail. But you can do me one favour, marshal."

"I'll do anything."

"I'll need a fresh horse."

"You can have mine. It's stabled back of here. I'll get it saddled up and . . ."

"You get into your bunk marshal. I can do that."

Catsfoot held out his hand. Slowly, the marshal gripped it.

"Is there . . . is there anything more I can do, Catsfoot?"

"Yes," he said simply. "If Janamo finishes me, will you

promise one thing? Will you get the soldiers to go after him, no matter how long it takes and no matter who tries to stop you?" He was moving towards the door as he added quietly: "If I do have to die, I wouldn't like it to be for nothing. . . ."

Before he went out into the night, he turned and waved to the marshal. He was smiling again.

Somehow the marshal managed to smile, too, as he waved back.

There was no hint of danger. Not to any ordinary man.

The faint breeze, warming to a new day, carried only soft gurgling sounds from the Gila River. The place where Catsfoot had been resting seemed to be enclosed in an eternity of peace.

Seemed to be. . . .

But Catsfoot knew that from somewhere in the Arizona wilderness danger was approaching. He knew it because a sixth sense he possessed had broken his sleep. He had been awakened suddenly by this inexplicable power of his—a power which had many times saved his own life and the lives of others.

He had left the trail route soon after leaving Tucson, using the remaining hours of darkness to ride hard across unmarked territory. This was worthwhile because it cut the distance to Meditation by nearly forty miles.

By dawn, he had reached the banks of the slow-flowing Gila. After swimming his horse across it, he had camped.

Sheltered by a cluster of mesquite shrubs, with a single long blanket folded under and over him, he had fallen into a light sleep.

Three hours passed. The sun climbed. Then the warning came, tingling his nerve-ends. . . .

Catsfoot did not move when he opened his eyes. Instead, he lay completely still and relaxed. He knew that before he could act intelligently he must first locate the exact danger area. He also knew that if he were patient and waited, something to be seen or heard would eventually pin-point the place for him.

The waiting lasted less than a minute.

It ended with the sudden soaring of an eagle.

The bird rose hurriedly and almost vertically from the line of cliffs, which were facing Catsfoot and a mile to the south. It circled high. It winged low. Then it rose to circle again. But it did not attempt to return to its nesting place, which must be in a rock fissure. Obviously, it had been disturbed. But by what? No animal was likely to disturb the eagle in its remote eyrie. But the arrival of men might do so.

Catsfoot stood up. His eyes seldom left the cliffs and the bird as he rolled his blanket, strapped on his gun belt and re-saddled the horse.

He was tightening the girth strap when the bird alighted on a pinnacle and seemed to be staring towards the ground on the other side of the cliffs.

Shielding his eyes, Catsfoot looked at the cliff formation very carefully. It was a familiar feature of the territory. Like the one remaining wall of some gigantic fortification, it rose sheer out of the ground to a height varying from a hundred to three hundred feet. From end to end it measured about a quarter of a mile.

Because he was directly facing it, Catsfoot could not see any of the ground behind the formation. But he was confident that it concealed a shallow valley, probably well sprinkled with rocks. They almost always occurred on one side of such geological barriers.

Catsfoot thought: "I've got to get to Meditation—and get there as fast as I can. I don't know who's behind those cliffs and I don't care. I'm keeping clear of them. . . ."

But the strangers, whoever they were, would be certain to see him as he rode past—unless he made a wide detour. He decided against the detour. It would take up far too much time. Instead, he would compromise. He would keep a moderate distance away from the rocks as he passed them, to have enough start to get easily away if the strangers showed too much interest in him.

He bore to his right, so as to have several hundred yards between himself and the edge of the barrier when he drew level with it. And he held the horse to a slow, quiet walking pace.

Again, he asked himself questions and sought logical answers. Who would the strangers be?

They must be either whites or Apaches. But very few whites ever crossed this part of the territory. The land was too rough for ordinary travel. It was too poor for stock-raising. And there was no copper to be mined in these parts.

So it seemed likely that they were Apaches. For here, Apache bands were not uncommon. They sometimes used the remoteness of the place to regroup and recover after attacks on the railroad which, at its nearest point, was only twenty-five miles away.

" Yes, it's almost certain they'll be Indians," Catsfoot thought. " And I'm not going to tangle with them! But I don't think they'll do anything when they see they haven't any chance of catching me."

Now he was level with the cliffs.

They loomed five hundred yards away, on his left.

Turning in the saddle, still riding very slowly, Catsfoot examined the land behind the barrier.

Yes, a valley, as he had expected. And in it there were scatterings of boulders, some as big as homesteads and others little larger than a man's fist.

It was an exceptionally shallow valley. Hardly more than a dip in the ground. Which made it easy to see and count the Apaches.

Five Apaches.

Five grouped in the centre of the valley where, it seemed, they were talking very seriously to each other. Their ponies were cropping the wiry grass some distance from them.

They did not offer the slightest danger. Of that, Catsfoot was more certain than ever. If they did attempt to give chase, his already long start would be further increased while they were running to their ponies.

But that tension remained. The feeling that the unexpected was about to become the unavoidable.

Now the Apaches had seen him. . . .

For a mere moment, Catsfoot glimpsed five faces turned in his direction. Then there was a short violent movement among the little group. And there were only four faces. It was as if one of them had suddenly taken cover behind the others. Or had been thrust there.

Five . . .? Four . . .?

Catsfoot's brain jolted to the truth. A truth which it had barely had time to absorb. Four of those faces were the colour of dark bronze. The other had a much lighter tan. Four wore Apache suede pelts round their foreheads and under their long black hair. The other did not wear a pelt. They had been too closely grouped for Catsfoot to notice the fifth man's clothes. But he was sure they were not those of an Apache.

Number five was a white! A white man in the hands of four Apaches. That sudden movement had been caused when they hid him from Catsfoot's eyes.

Catsfoot turned his head away from the Indians. At the slow walking pace, he rode on. Rode past the rock formation and the shallow valley. He continued south, towards Meditation, as if he had noticed nothing unusual. Or as if, in any case, he did not care.

In fact, he was enduring a spell of painful indecision.

To reach Meditation, to call out Janamo, that was the whole reason for his crossing this territory. But the longer he delayed, the farther Janamo was likely to drift from Meditation and he could not stay away from his commissions as a trail scout for too long. Hours counted. And who could guess how long it might take to investigate the presence of a white man among the Apaches?

He crested a rise in the ground. The valley fell out of sight behind him while he argued with himself.

It was by no means certain that the white man was not perfectly satisfied to be with the Apaches. He might be one of a small number who did a lucrative business with the Indians, trading guns and liquor to them. If that were so, the man himself would not want to be seen by a passing rider. So he would have deliberately hidden himself behind the others.

But what if he were a captive of the redskins?

It was not a pleasant thought. Of all the Indian races, none was more consistently and hideously cruel to captured enemies than the thirteen sects which made up the Apaches. Their prisoners died. But they took a long time to do so.

If he were a prisoner, it would be unthinkable to leave him. At least an attempt would have to be made to rescue him.

With the valley far behind and invisible, Catsfoot did what, in his heart, he had known from the beginning he would have to do. He turned his horse so as to re-approach the place in a wide semi-circle.

To return without being seen or heard called for the very detour which he had previously avoided. It called for two hours of hard riding, ending in another slow, cautious approach.

He and the horse were drenched with sweat when they again approached the cliff formation. Again the Apaches were on the other side of the jagged barrier.

Catsfoot dismounted and haltered the animal under the shadow of the sheer rocks.

On foot, he assumed the swift, noiseless, feline quality which had given him his name. No cougar on the hunt could have moved with a more deadly certainty. Keeping close to the base of the rocks, he seemed to blend with them, becoming visible only in brief flashes. He stopped when he reached the end of the formation, which was no more than thirty feet wide. Turning the angle of the rocks, he pressed his back to them, easing sideways.

He stopped when the Apaches and the white man came into view.

Then Catsfoot knew that he had been right to return.

The Apaches had not moved from the centre of the valley. But now they were less than a hundred paces away. And they were sprawling on the ground where, judging by the refuse around them, they had just finished a meal of meat and pemmican biscuit.

They were young braves. And at least three of them were well-armed. For beside them lay a couple of the new Winchester fifteen-round repeating rifles and a .52 Spencer repeating carbine, designed to take seven rounds of the very heavy ammunition. Catsfoot was not so sure about the equipment of the fourth brave. He had a revolver, which he was checking and reloading. In every way it looked like an ordinary Colt Frontier. It was designed to look like a Colt Frontier. But when the Apache spun the cylinder Catsfoot knew that it had not been made by the famous Connecticut gun-makers. A genuine Colt—like any other good revolver—produced a soft whirring sound when the cylinder was spun. A sound which was proof of perfectly machined parts made of the finest steel. But the Apache's gun made a harsh, grating noise. Catsfoot suspected that it was a cheap, imitation Colt. Many of these were available.

Catsfoot noted and assessed these facts about the Apaches' equipment within a few seconds. Then his gaze fixed on the white man, who was sitting a little apart from the redskins.

He had been a well-built man, that white.

It was easy to guess that, until very recently, he had been in the prime of a vigorous and confident life. Now he was a pathetic husk. A shaking, quavering, terrified wreck.

His shirt, torn and grimy, revealed folds of loose skin where there must have been hard muscle. His unshaven and unwashed face was prematurely old, the lips turning inward, the cheeks sunken. And the eyes seemed to reflect all the agonies known to mankind. They were gazing with horror on the Apaches.

Yet he bore no sign of physical ill-treatment. No wounds, no bruises.

Puzzled, Catsfoot thought: "He can't have been in Apache hands for long. If he had, he'd be looking even worse. So how has he got himself into this state? He must have been like this when the Apaches got hold of him. Can he be ill . . .?"

The Apaches were getting to their feet. They were grouping round the quaking white, smiling as they looked down upon him, his helpless terror causing them great amusement.

One of the Apaches bent down, put his hands under the captive's armpits, and effortlessly jerked him upright. He swayed, recovered, then stood with his head hung down and his twitching hands clasped together, as if silently pleading for mercy.

The Apache began speaking to him. He did so quietly, so that Catsfoot could pick up only occasional isolated words. They told him no more than that the brave was speaking in both English and his native Mescalero patois, which was the usual Apache method of addressing whites.

The man seemed to understand for he slowly raised his head and shook it.

Then, in a croaking shout, he exclaimed: "No! I can't! Y'know I can't!"

The four young Apaches laughed, nudging each other to stress their amusement.

The one who seemed to be their leader pulled a hunting knife from his waist sash. It had a thin, nine-inch blade which tapered to a needle-sharp point. The handle was ivory. It was a superb weapon, deadly yet beautiful. The Apache fondled it. Then, with a flick of his wrist, he threw it at the ground. It buried itself to the hilt in the hard soil.

The Apache leader turned. He walked away from the knife, appearing to count his strides as he did so. He walked towards the cliff formation.

The Apache completed twenty careful paces. He stopped. And he turned again, so that he was facing the partly buried knife.

Meanwhile, another redskin had measured a further twenty paces in the opposite direction. This was the brave who owned the imitation Colt Frontier. He marked a spot with a foot. Then, protesting feebly, the white man was pulled and pushed towards that spot.

Now Catsfoot knew exactly what was intended. The scene was being set for a form of duelling common to many Indian peoples. At a given signal, each man rushed for the knife. Then they fought—until one died. The greatest advantage lay with the faster runner, for he gained the weapon.

But this . . .

This could not be a real duel. The white would have no chance. He could scarcely stand and certainly he could not run and fight.

A probable explanation suddenly occurred to Catsfoot. But he did not ponder upon it. There was no time for that. The moment had come when he must play his own part in the cruel drama. . . .

He lifted his Dragoons from their holsters, thumbed back the hammers. Holding the guns at waist level, he glided forward. He turned round the side of the cliffs and entered the valley.

The three Apaches who were farthest away were the first to see Catsfoot. Laughing, taunting, they were giving the white his duelling orders. Then abruptly their voices died. They stared glazedly at the tall man in buckskins, as if a ghost had materialised from the rocks.

Their captive stared, too. Then he put a trembling hand to his eyes. He looked again, peeping through the fingers, as though wanting to believe that Catsfoot was there but fearing that this was a trick of the imagination.

The Apache leader had his back to Catsfoot and was well to one side of him. For seconds he watched the others and looked no more than slightly puzzled. Then, directed by their gaze, he half-turned. Immediately he recoiled a step, like a man driven back by a body blow. His bronzed and cruel young face grew creases of fear. He retreated another step as Catsfoot moved towards him to make sure that he was unarmed. Satisfied on that point without needing to touch him, Catsfoot began walking the forty yards towards the others.

Those three other Apaches could be dangerous. Two of them had Winchester repeaters under their arms, the third had the cheap revolver under his sash. And they had had time to recover from their first shock.

When he had covered half the distance, Catsfoot stopped. He made a downward movement with his Dragoons. Its meaning was clear in any language. But he emphasised it by saying slowly and clearly: "Drop your guns!"

They hesitated. Catsfoot eased down the hammers of his Dragoons. Then he quickly re-cocked them. Against the background of silence, the softly menacing clicks were heard plainly.

That decided the Apaches. The Winchesters fell to the ground. A moment later the revolver followed.

Catsfoot smiled briefly at the gaping white and said: "You'd best come over here and stand with me."

The man reeled towards Catsfoot and he did the one thing that Catsfoot had not expected.

He swayed. At the same time, he flung his arms round Catsfoot's neck to save himself from falling.

The result was threefold. The sudden impact pushed Catsfoot momentarily off balance. The man's weight dragged Catsfoot's head down. The emaciated body inserted itself between Catsfoot's pair of Dragoons, so that they were put out of target alignment and could not be immediately re-sighted.

It was then that Catsfoot made a mistake—the mistake of being too gentle. Although he could not use his hands, he could very easily have broken the hold by a violent elbow jab between the ribs. But, because of the man's pathetic condition, he did not do that. Instead, he tried to back away and twist free.

It was useless. Although now only semi-conscious, the man clung on to Catsfoot with fanatical strength.

In desperation and sensing danger from the Apaches, Catsfoot hooked his left leg round one of the man's ankles and gave it a jerk. That did it. The man's hands slid free of Catsfoot's neck. He folded to the ground.

At the same moment Catsfoot felt a rush of air smite his cheek. He heard the shrieking of a heavy bullet travelling at maximum velocity, the rataplan crash of exploding powder. He felt pain as a fragment of stone, dislodged by the slug, hit him between the shoulder blades.

And he saw the leader of the Apaches.

The young brave was less than fifteen yards away. He was down on one knee. And the powerful Spencer repeating carbine was at his shoulder. He was thrusting the under-lever down and up, to bring another round into the breech from the carbine's tube magazine.

Catsfoot was dazed by the pain in his back. But he reacted immediately and instinctively. . . .

The crash from his two Dragoons came in the single fraction of a second. And they came as the Apache was thumbing back the hammer of his Spencer.

The Apache fired the Spencer. But he did so as the Dragoon slugs were entering his chest. He had already started to fall forward when his bullet left the muzzle of the carbine. It twisted into the earth close in front of the Apache, excavating a tunnel many feet deep.

But Catsfoot had already swung round to face the three others. He saw only two of them and they were picking up their Winchesters. His Dragoons parted slightly, each drawing a bead on a different target. His slugs tore into the breach casings of the Winchester. The repeaters were torn out of the hands of the two Apaches. One of them rose high in the air, the other spun along the ground. Neither would be usable again. And the Apaches were staring dumbly at broken fingers.

Where was the fourth and last Apache?

Catsfoot pirouetted a complete and lightning-fast circle, first pressure already on the triggers. He was not to be seen. So he must have taken cover behind one of the boulders. A glance at the ground showed Catsfoot that the Apache had recovered his imitation Colt.

Catsfoot knew that he must take cover, too. Standing here, he was an easy target. And he must get the white man under cover at the same time.

The white had fallen into a deep faint. He was sprawled on his back, eyes tight closed. He would have to be dragged behind the nearest boulder. Which meant that, despite the risk, Catsfoot would have to replace his guns in their holsters. There could be no advantage in continuing to hold the guns while he pulled the man over the ground. In that position, he would not be able to aim with them. And they would slow him down when speed was vital.

The holsters received Catsfoot's two smoking Dragoons.

He bent down and put his hands under the unconscious man's armpits.

That was as far as he got.

A shout of maniac fury came from close behind him. Only a few yards away. Much too close even for Catsfoot to have any hope of turning, drawing, aiming and firing while the Apache need only squeeze a trigger. The one slender chance was to avoid any sudden movement. . . .

Slowly, Catsfoot released his grip on the unconscious white. Equally slowly, he straightened up and turned. The Apache was kneeling on one of the smaller boulders. Savagery and a lust for vengeance was contorting his face. His gun was aimed directly between Catsfoot's eyes. And, unlike most Indians, he knew plenty about using a gun. Catsfoot knew that by the way he was holding the revolver. His arm was fully extended in the orthodox fire position, which was the best for all except the supreme experts.

With his free hand, the Apache gestured towards his dead friend. Then he pointed accusingly at Catsfoot, his bloodshot eyes rolling.

With the gun still accurately sighted on Catsfoot, and at close range, he squeezed the trigger. The hammer fell. There was a very faint, sickly report. Like the bursting of a partly inflated paper bag. That was all. No bullet screeched out of the muzzle.

Catsfoot knew what had happened—and what was likely to happen if the Indian tried to fire again. He shouted a warning. And his own guns leapt into his hands. But already the Apache had flipped back the hammer and was once more squeezing the trigger.

A double explosion came from the Apache's gun. They almost, but not quite, came together. Then something occurred which was ghastly and weird. The gun barrel seemed to swell like a balloon. And it burst as Catsfoot threw himself to the ground. Burning powder scorched the Apache's face, slivers of jagged steel cut into his right arm and shoulder. He screamed as he rolled from the rock.

Catsfoot rushed to him, pulled off his doe-skin jacket. A quick examination showed him that the Apache had been very lucky. None of the wounds was deep or serious. The steel fragments which had caused them could safely wait until they were removed by his own people. And the facial burns, although painful, would soon heal.

Catsfoot murmured to himself: "I never thought I'd owe my life to a hang-fire—but that's how it's been!"

Hang-fire . . .

The word was familiar to all Westerners who handled guns. A hang-fire was very different and more dangerous than a misfire. The misfire was harmless. It was a total failure of the primer to detonate the powder behind the bullet.

But in the case of a hang-fire, one of two things happened. Sometimes there would be a delay of anything up to three minutes between the hammer falling and the cartridge exploding. Or—and this had happened to the Apache—only a tiny fraction of the powder would explode, producing a faint, and occasionally unnoticeable bang. In this case, the force was just sufficient to push the bullet out of the cartridge case and into the barrel, where it remained. That was why Catsfoot, realising what had happened, had shouted his warning. For when the Apache fired his second shot he had blasted one bullet into the back of another. In a good gun, this was not usually too serious. The rifling inside the barrel suffered, and that was all. But the Apache's junk, imitation Colt had proved incapable of withstanding the double strain. It had burst. The main danger of both forms of hang-fire was that they could easily be mistaken for a simple misfire.

Turning round, Catsfoot looked at the two other surviving Apaches. They were holding their damaged fingers under their arms. They avoided Catsfoot's gaze as he walked towards them. He stopped when only a few inches from them.

"You can both count yourselves lucky to be alive," he said. "The same's true of your friend with the bad gun. I'm going to let the three of you go. But before I do that, I want something from you—I want to know how you got hold of this white man and why you were going to force him into a knife fight! Talk fast and talk right! If you tell me any lies, I might change my mind about letting you go free!"

Neither of the young braves attempted to answer. They continued to nurse their fingers and stare at the ground.

Very slowly, Catsfoot lifted his left gun. He pressed it deep into the stomach of one of the Apaches, at the same time cocking the hammer. His normally kindly eyes had become chippings of pale blue ice. His voice came from between closed teeth.

" Talk . . .! Talk, unless you want to be silent for always!"

The Apache's resistance broke. In a mixture of English and his own patois, he spoke. His story came slowly at first, then in a wild torrent . . .

The four of them had been disgraced by their tribe. Told to hunt for food while their elders attacked the railroad, they had disobeyed their orders. Wanting to share in the glory of war, they had opened fire on a gang of railroad labourers a few miles west of Tucson. The labourers, they had thought, were unarmed and helpless. In fact they were neither. The labourers had grabbed guns from the side of the rail tracks and returned the fire.

Shocked and suddenly very scared, the four young Apaches had broken cover and raced for their ponies. But the labourers, who were no fools when it came to fighting, cut off their retreat with enfilade fire.

They were rescued by pure chance. It happened that a large Apache war party was in the area and heard the shots. They drove the labourers back—but only after several experienced braves had been killed.

Back at their encampment, the four were condemned as rebels and cowards. Their punishment was traditional—to wander as outcasts until each, by some action of gallantry, atoned.

They wandered for weeks. Then, the previous day, they came across a wreck of a white man who seemed also to be wandering. The white put up no resistance when they swooped upon him.

Looking at this helpless man, their leader saw a way of restoring his reputation. If he could say to his people that he had out-fought a white in a knife duel. . . . And if he could produce the white's scalp as evidence. . . . Then surely he would be forgiven. . . .

The arrival of Catsfoot had prevented what would have been nothing other than a merciless, calculated murder.

The explanation for the fight was the one which had occurred to Catsfoot. And now that it was confirmed, he felt bitter at the thought that he must let these three go unpunished. But, short of encumbering himself with three Apache prisoners, there was nothing else he could do.

Half an hour later, after their leader had been buried, he watched them ride out of the valley.

Then he turned anxiously to the man who had been their prisoner. That man, now lying on Catsfoot's blanket, had regained consciousness. But the shadows in his eyes told Catsfoot that his end was near.

Catsfoot knelt beside him and gave him water from his canteen. Then he asked: "Who are you? Where do you come from?"

The man stared blankly at Catsfoot and remained silent.

"Try to talk," Catsfoot said gently. "Tell me who you are."

This time his lips trembled. In a whisper, he answered.

"I was . . . was a lawman once," he said. "A deputy . . . a deputy marshal."

"Where were you a deputy?"

"Place called . . . called Tarran Butts . . . Janamo's men gunned me . . . gunned me down . . . I've still got the bullet in me . . . listen and listen good 'cause I ain't got . . . got much longer for talkin'. . . ."

His name was Matt Swade and he had been one of nine deputies who stood and fought with their marshal when Janamo rode into Tarran.

Matt saw two of his fellow deputies shot by Janamo's men. He saw the marshal out-gunned by Janamo in a set fight. Then Matt's nerve had broken. Instead of surrendering like the others, he had tried to run wildly, crazily, out of town. A bullet brought him down.

For nearly a month he had been cared for by the doctor in Tarran. It was when the doctor eventually told him that the bullet was in too deep to be removed that Matt reached his decision. Since he was going to die anyway, he would try to make amends for running away by riding to Tucson in an attempt to fetch help.

Half-delirious with fever, he had risen unseen from his sickbed, saddled his horse, and left the town in the early hours of one morning.

It was amazing that he had got so far towards Tucson before the young Apaches found him. . . .

Just before he died Matt Swade whispered: " Don't never cross . . . cross Janamo's path . . . that Mexie's so . . . so fast it don't seem real . . . it's like as if the devil hisself was drawin' a gun. . . ."

CHAPTER FOUR

Duel with fear

EVIL, hideous, the vulture part-closed its shaggy wings and dropped low over Meditation.

It flapped noisily past Abe Solomon's mercantile store and Pat O'Toole's rooming house.

Descending yet farther, it cast beady eyes at the saloon where Buddy Lane, the owner, was talking urgently to a crowd of attentive customers.

It flew into the deserted blacksmith's shop and alighted briefly on to the cold forge.

Before departing, the bird of prey circled a battered framewood building from which the notice *Meditation Gazette* had been torn down and pushed through a window.

The vulture was one of many which had been keeping vigil over the town for days. Sensing disaster, they had winged in from the Yuma Desert, hoping to find rich pickings for themselves. They had been disappointed. But they had not given up. Each dawn they came and they did not depart until twilight. They went on hoping for the death of the town.

But Meditation continued to live—sometimes dazedly, sometimes hysterically, like a wounded animal which survives because instinct dictates that it must. And, like any wounded animal, the town was capable of ferocious madnesses. Such as the madness which was being encouraged by Buddy Lane in his saloon. . . .

Buddy, elegantly draped in a blue velveteen jacket and waving a cheroot in his long holder, was standing on a chair to address the crowd.

The leading member of the Town Committee, Buddy was a persuasive speaker. He was using all those powers now.

" So it comes to this, folks," he was saying, " we no sooner

get rid of Janamo than Ralph Lucas plans to have him back!
He's talkin' about a newspaper campaign against the Mexicans!
What'd that mean? I'll tell you—it'd mean we'd have the
whole durned lot of them here again, as soon as they heard
about it!"

There was a rumble of uneasy agreement. But a copper miner
said: "That don't make sense to me. Lucas ain't got no
noospaper no more! Ain't all that print machinery of his been
smashed to perdition?"

Buddy smoothed his glossy black head and smiled knowingly.

"You've been out of the town, workin' that claim of yours,"
he said. "So it seems you haven't heard how hard Lucas has
been workin' these last few days on repairs. He told me himself the damage ain't near so bad as he expected. The Mexies
spent most of the time pullin' the steam motor apart. *That's*
finished for good. But he can do without it! The printer can be
turned by hand when he's done mendin' it! He's talkin' about
havin' the *Gazette* out again in a week, with a load of yap on
the front page about bringin' Janamo to justice! Think what
that'd mean, folks! How long before Janamo pays us another
call if we let Lucas go ahead? And y'know what? Janamo won't
go so easy on us next time! He . . ."

Abe Solomon, who had left his daughter in charge of his
store, shouted indignantly from the back of the crowd: "He
didn't go so easy *last* time! I've had half my stock looted!
And all the money from my cash drawers!"

"Yep, but that's nothin' to what he'll do if he's been made
mad by Lucas!" Buddy retorted. "Last time, just one man was
killed. That's because all of us 'cept poor Harry Fost and Will
Hambert acted sensible. How many'll they gun down after
Lucas has insulted them? I tell you, folks, none of us'll be safe!"

There was a rumble of agreement. But not from all of them.
A few were uncomfortably silent.

One of Buddy's barmen, straining to curry favour, asked:
"What d'you want us to do? Tell us and we'll do it!"

"I'll tell you," Buddy said. "We'll all go to see Lucas right now! We'll let him know we're not goin' to risk our skins again just because of his crazy idea! We'll tell him he's not even to mention Janamo in the *Gazette*!"

A rancher asked: "Supposin' he don't listen to us?"

There was an expectant hush. Every eye was on Buddy, who had been hoping for this question and did not rush his answer. He paused dramatically, making a broad gesture with his cheroot. Then he said very slowly: "If Lucas won't do like we tell him, we'll just have to fix things so he won't be able to do no harm! We'll have to do the job Janamo didn't finish! We'll wreck that print machine of his so it'll never work again, even if he sweats on it for twenty years!"

A gentle hiss of escaping breath came from the crowd. Normally law-abiding, the suggestion momentarily shocked them.

"That'd make us the same as Janamo's gang," Solomon said.

"No, it won't! We'll only get tough if we have to! It's up to Lucas. If he acts wise, nobody'll harm his property. . . ." Buddy bent forward on the chair and shouted, "This could be life or death for us, folks! If we let Lucas bait Janamo back here, a whole lot of us won't live long enough to weep no tears about what happens! Are you comin' with me to see Lucas?"

There was a roar of assent. Buddy Lane got off the chair. As he pushed through the crowd, many hands slapped him on the back. He had succeeded in thoroughly frightening them, so they were ready to follow him in almost anything.

With the dandified and crafty saloon keeper at their head, the crowd streamed along the main street, making for the offices of the *Meditation Gazette*.

Lucas was very tired, but very pleased.

Leaning against a tall case of shelves, he looked at massed rows of printing type—thousands of alphabetically arranged metal letters, all graded in various sizes.

A few days earlier, most of that type had been scattered over the floor by Janamo's men. Retrieving it and reassembling it in the right order had been a back-breaking and tedious task, but a vital preliminary before there could be any hope of again publishing the *Gazette*. Now, at last, it was done.

" I've finished," he said. " How are you doing, Bason?"

The fat Bason Thebes stopped working on the flat-bed printing machine. He had been bolting a handle to the gears, so that the machine could be hand-driven now that the steam motor had been smashed beyond repair.

" This is about ready as well, Mister Lucas."

Lucas wiped ink from his hands with a kerosene-soaked rag.

" The stage coach ought to be back from Tucson in a couple of days with a package of agency news reports from the east," he said. " Then we can start preparing the paper—we'll be in business again. But right now, I'm going to start writing my piece about Janamo."

His round eyes absurdly serious, oil in upstanding hair, Bason trundled towards Lucas.

Watching him, Lucas recognised the signs. It was obvious from his pudding-shaped face that Bason Thebes was about to disgorge another of his thunderous lies. He had been oddly quiet since the time the Mexicans had wrecked the office, but now he was recovering.

" Did I ever tell you about the time I was personal bodyguard to President Grant and the . . ."

Bason stopped because Lucas was not even pretending to be interested. Lucas had moved to the open door and was looking along the street.

Puzzled and vaguely uneasy, Lucas watched the crowd approach. He noted Buddy Lane in the lead and apparently in some sort of authority. Lucas, who got on well with most people, had never been able to like Buddy. To him, the saloon keeper had always seemed as trustworthy as a house-trained rattlesnake.

The original crowd was being reinforced by other townsfolk. It came to a shuffling stop in front of the *Gazette* office. Every face was turned towards Lucas.

Buddy jumped on to the boardwalk. As he halted opposite Lucas, he wore an expression of outraged innocence.

"We wanta talk to you, Lucas," Buddy said, keeping his voice up for the benefit of his audience.

"I'm listening."

"You're goin' to start printin' your paper again soon—that right?"

"Sure. The next edition'll be out in a few days. Printing will take longer than usual because the steam motor is not . . ."

"Never mind the steam motor! Is it right you plan to publish hard things about Janamo?"

"I certainly do!"

"Such as what?"

"Such as a demand for immediate action against him and his gang!"

"Very nice!" Buddy said, curling his lips. "D'you mind tellin' us what sort of action exactly?"

"I want the law to act, if that's possible. But if it isn't, I'm going to suggest that every town in this part of the territory contributes ten of its best men towards a posse to hunt down Janamo. That way, we'd get together a posse of at least a hundred guns and . . ."

Buddy interrupted. Pushing his hands deep into the pockets of his velveteen jacket, he shouted: "You crazy idjit! You stupid, dangerous yip! D'you *wanta* bring them riders back here? D'you *want* more killin', more lootin'? Don't y'know that's what'll happen if we let you print that sorta stuff!"

Confused shouts of agreement came from the crowd. Momentarily taken aback, Lucas blinked at them then at Buddy.

"Yes, Janamo may come back," Lucas agreed. "But this time, we can be ready for him! We can organise to drive him off before he gets into Meditation. We have plenty of men and plenty of guns for that. Day and night look-outs can be organised, so we have plenty of warning, and we . . ."

"You're stark mad!" Buddy cut in. "You expect the folks here to get themselves killed so you can print sensations in your yeller news sheet! Nobody in this burgh's goin' to commit suicide just to please you, Lucas!"

There were renewed shouts of approval. This time, they

were louder and wilder. People were joining the crowd from all parts of the town and they were forming a half-circle thirty-deep round the front of the building. Looking at their malevolent faces, Lucas felt as if he had suddenly been betrayed and attacked by people whom he had thought were friends.

"A fight for justice can't be suicide!" Lucas replied. He tried to speak loudly, but his voice was not strong. It sounded thin and unconvincing in comparison to Buddy's. "Resistance to Janamo's got to begin somewhere, unless we're going to be picked off one by one, like a bunch of tame rabbits!" he added.

"Talk! Just cheap talk!" shouted Buddy, who was himself probably the most prolific talking man in Meditation. "Well, you're not goin' to do it, Lucas! You're not goin' to print that kinda stuff!"

"Aren't I? And who says so?"

"We all say so! We want you to give y'word you're not even goin' to mention Janamo's name in your paper, Lucas! And we want you to give it to us now—here and now, with everybody listenin'!"

Lucas felt the familiar flush of anger hit his cheeks.

"I won't be told by you or anyone else what I'll print in the Gazette! Janamo tried that and he failed! You're going to do no better!"

Trying to look tough, encouraged by the thought that the crowd was with him while Lucas was alone, Buddy shouted: "If that's the way y'feel, we'll take this office of yours apart! We'll do better than Janamo—we'll burn down the whole durned building with the print machinery inside it!"

Lucas felt dank, bitter despair. He tasted the special agony of those who are threatened by the very people they are trying to defend. Against Janamo, an enemy, he had been able to show courage. Against these townsfolk, his friends, he was helpless.

"I'll write what I like, or nothing at all," he said. "Smash the *Gazette* if you like, but if you do, the time'll come when you . . ."

His words were drowned by a roar from the crowd.

Buddy turned to face them.

"You all heard him!" he screamed. "It's his own fault! Let's make a fire out of the place!"

The crowd of normally peaceful people had become a frenzied mob, spurred not by any dislike of Lucas, but by fear for themselves. They wavered for a few moments, swaying back and forward, as if moved by a breeze.

Then, with a renewed roar, they rushed towards the *Gazette* office. Buddy, brave because of the mob's support, pushed Lucas aside and made for the entrance. He reached the doorway. Some of those following him got as far as the boardwalk.

But no farther.

Suddenly, all of them stopped. They halted as if visited by lightning paralysis.

The reverberating crash of two guns did it.

The guns—and the iced menace of a man's voice which came from the middle of the street as the last, hollow echo was fading.

"If any of you tries to enter that building, he'll stop a .44 slug," the voice told them.

Slowly, fearfully, like people in a nightmare, the crowd turned.

They saw a tall and slender man in buckskins sitting a powerful chestnut stallion. A man whose flaxen hair fell to his shoulders. A man who was holding a Colt Dragoon in each hand. Thin spirals of smoke were drifting idly from the muzzles of the guns. They were being held forward from the waist and aimed rock-steady at Buddy Lane's chest.

For tense seconds, they remained still.

Buddy Lane broke the trance. Seeing the aim of the guns, noting the cocked hammers, and with the thick sweat of fear erupting from his brow, he shifted away from the door. Trembling, Buddy hopped from the boardwalk to the road. There he tried to lose himself among the others.

Still holding the Dragoons, Catsfoot swung a leg over the saddle until he was sitting sideways on it. Then he jumped easily to the ground. With his long, graceful strides he seemed to glide through the crowd and they melted apart to make way for him.

As Catsfoot reached the boardwalk he replaced his guns in their holsters and moved up to Lucas.

" Would you be the man who owns the town newspaper?" he asked.

" That's right. My name's Ralph Lucas."

And as he spoke, Lucas was surprised to find that he was not in the least afraid of this tall stranger in buckskins. Looking into the calm eyes, he sensed a man who could be ruthless—but only to his enemies. And they were the eyes of a man who would not willingly make an enemy of anyone.

Lucas thought: " Whoever he is, this stranger can be dangerous—but not to me and not to people like me. . . ."

But aloud, Lucas added: " I'm glad you happened along. My offices were going to be burnt down."

" I'm glad I could help. Folks call me Catsfoot." Catsfoot put out a hand.

As Lucas clasped the proffered hand, he said hesitantly: " You're . . . you would be Catsfoot the trail scout?"

" The same."

Lucas blinked and said excitedly: " I didn't expect I'd ever meet *you*! I've heard plenty about you, of course. But I never thought you'd arrive in a place like Meditation? What's brought you here?"

" That's something I'd like to talk to you about."

" We can do that in my office."

Lucas nodded towards the open door and stood aside.

The townsfolk had been listening open-mouthed. Some of them heard Catsfoot introduce himself and his name was repeated in awed whispers. As the two men vanished into the *Gazette* office, the crowd began slowly to break up and move away, talking in semi-stupefied little groups.

Catsfoot paused just inside the office. He looked at the counter from which copies of the paper were sold, at the printing department just beyond, and at the open-fronted horse stall which had become Lucas's editorial office. His gaze drifted back to the printing machine. It seemed to interest him.

" Never been in one of these places before," he said. " Mebbe sometime you'll show me how you print a newspaper?"

" Glad to. It's quite simple. But from now on, printing's going to take a long time because Janamo and his men smashed the steam motor. Still, we've fixed it so we can operate by hand power."

" You say ' we ' fixed it—you've got help?"

" I have an assistant who . . ."

At that moment, a trap-door opened in the centre of the floor. The spiky hair and round face of Bason Thebes made a cautious appearance. He blinked round, saw Lucas and gave a weak smile.

" Where . . . where's the crowd?" he asked.

" Gone," Lucas told him.

" They've not done any damage?"

" None at all. Catsfoot, here, came along in time. He pushed them off."

Bason's portly shape rose from the opening in the floor. He tried to look casual.

" Catsfoot? Say—are you Catsfoot the gunfighter and trail scout?"

For just a moment Catsfoot looked mildly annoyed.

" I'm a trail scout, but I don't like being called a gunfighter."

Bason, too stupid to notice that he had caused offence, blundered on: " It's easy for professional gunslingers like us to handle that sort of mob!"

" Is it?" Catsfoot asked. " You can use a gun, can you?"

Bason screwed up his face into a scowl which was meant to look tough. In fact, it only succeeded in being fatly ridiculous.

" *Use* a gun! You're asking me?" Bason asked with bitter scorn. " Listen, Catsfoot, I reckon I'm the fastest gun in the New territories . . . d'you know Billy the Kid?"

Catsfoot raised his eyebrows at hearing the name of the infamous young killer.

"He's no friend of mine, but I've heard about him."

"Billy the Kid's fast with his gun."

"So they say."

Nodding seriously, Bason announced: "I outdrew Billy the Kid in a gunfight last year in Tombstone!"

Lucas gave Catsfoot a quick wink. It confirmed Catsfoot's suspicion that he was talking to a harmless liar.

"So you outdrew Billy the Kid, did you?" Catsfoot said, keeping his face straight. "That really is something. You sure must be fast with your gun."

"There's none faster than me," Bason smirked. "Not even you, Catsfoot."

"All the same, it seems you can't shoot straight."

Bason's round eyes glittered furiously.

"Me not shoot straight. . . .! I can snuff out a candle-wick at thirty paces! I once clipped a wing off a fly at ten paces!"

Enjoying himself, Catsfoot said smoothly: "But you must have missed Billy the Kid when you had that fight with him, because he's still alive and well. He's never even been wounded at any time."

Bason was taken aback—but only momentarily.

"Oh . . . yep . . . yep, well that's because of the goodness of m'heart. I had him helpless, but I just didn't want to squeeze the trigger. While he stood there trembling and at my mercy, I told him to mend his ways. Then I let him go."

Catsfoot gave up. Lucas took over. He asked Bason: "Where did you get to when the crowd looked like breaking in this office? Your fast, straight shooting would have been durned useful right then."

Bason fluttered his podgy hands.

"Gee, I sure do wish I'd been with you," he said apologetically. "But I was fetchin' my gun."

"Fetching your gun!"

"That's right, Mister Lucas. I figured I might need it. I could see the crowd might turn real mean."

"But you've just come out of the cellar!"

"I keep a gun in the cellar, Mister Lucas."

"You do? Where is it then? You haven't a gun with you now."

"I left it there when I heard the crowd move off. I knew there was no need for gunplay, after all."

Breathing hard, Lucas said: "It's a great comfort to have you around in times of danger, Bason."

Bason grinned modestly.

"Aw, think nothin' of it, sir." Bason turned to Catsfoot and added: "If I can give you any tips on gunplay, let me know. I'm always willin' to pass on my knowledge."

Lucas felt a surge of annoyance. For himself, he was willing to tolerate any amount of Bason's nonsense. But this was almost an insult to a visitor. He was relieved to see that Catsfoot was not taking offence.

"Thanks," Catsfoot said. "That's nice to know. I'd appreciate a few lessons from you when you can spare the time."

"Any time you like," Bason said, slapping his protruding stomach and glowing with satisfaction.

"Then how about right now?"

"Er . . . well . . ."

"Mebbe you'll show me how to speed up my double-draw. Fetch that gun of yours, Bason, and we'll have a friendly competition. We won't shoot to kill, of course. Just to wound."

Bason's eyes became glazed. He stared aghast at Catsfoot. His round face began to shake as if being massaged by an invisible hand.

"N-not t-to kill?" he croaked.

"That's what I said."

"J-just to w-wound?"

"You've got the idea, Bason. Of course, a mistake's always possible. A half-inch one way or the other can mean the difference between a nice, clean, simple wound and a killing . . . but I don't have to tell a gunfighter like *you* about that."

"It's t-too risky!"

"But *you* won't be running any risk," Catsfoot said soothingly, while Lucas blew his nose hard, his face hidden in a handkerchief. "Like you said, you can outdraw me, so I'll be the one to stop the slug. I figure it'll be worth while, just to be able to see a gunfighter like you in action."

Bason saw a way of escape. Partly recovering, he said: " I won't do it, Catsfoot. I don't want to risk doin' you a serious hurt—or even killin' you! "

Catsfoot sighed like a very disappointed man.

" I'm real sorry," he said. " I might have learnt a lot from you. But I can see now why you let Billy the Kid escape. You're too good-hearted, Bason."

And Bason glowed again, managing a modest shrug.

Lucas put away his handkerchief and said to Catsfoot: " Bason has work to do on the printing machine. We'll go into my office. . . ."

" I'll have to see to my horse first," Catsfoot said, glancing through the doorway to where the animal was standing un-attended in the street.

" Bason will do that. Come on, Catsfoot. . . ."

Lucas led the way past the shelves of type, the printing machine with its wrecked steam motor and the steel-topped tables where the pages were assembled. They sat on opposite sides of the desk in the converted stall. There they talked until deep into the afternoon.

It was a strange discussion. The backgrounds of the two young men could scarcely have been more different. Yet they quickly found a common bond in their hatred of all tyranny and in their belief that freedom and justice were worthy of any sacrifice.

Lucas was quickly aware of the quiet magnetism of Catsfoot, which had made the trail scout a legend in his lifetime. And, as they talked, Lucas became impressed by the way Catsfoot had painstakingly educated himself. Although he had never been to any school, Catsfoot had taught himself to read and was now familiar with American and English literature.

For his part, Catsfoot admired the editor's courage. And he felt something approaching awe on hearing that Lucas was a graduate of Harvard University.

But mainly they talked of Janamo. And when they finished, a decision had been reached.

They returned to the printing department, where Bason had completed the changes in the flat-bed machine.

With Catsfoot watching, Lucas pulled out a little-used drawer of extra large type. He worked for half an hour, assembling letters and carefully spacing them. Then he locked them tight in a steel frame, so that they could not fall out of place.

He took the type-loaded frame to the printing machine and bolted it under the ink rollers.

"Turn the handle," Lucas said to Bason.

Puzzled, Bason obeyed. A few seconds later, the three of them were looking at a large poster. It read:

GUN CHALLENGE TO JANAMO
CATSFOOT WAITS IN MEDITATION
FULL FACTS IN NEXT ISSUE OF *Gazette*

"I'll have these distributed over an area of a hundred miles," Lucas said. "The first of them can be pasted up right away in the town."

"They sure ought to bring Janamo in quickly," Catsfoot said.

"I only hope he doesn't arrive *too* quickly. We'll need a few days to get properly ready for him."

"That's a chance we'll have to take. The most important thing is for me to try to nail him before he and his mob can do any more killing."

Lucas said to Bason: "Run off two hundred of these posters."

Bason blinked and piped: "You want me to print two hundred! That's a big job, Mister Lucas, seein' I'll have to turn the machine by hand!"

"The exercise might get some of that fat off you! But don't worry—Catsfoot and I will help. When they're all printed, you can start posting some of them up in town. I'll pay stage operators and ranchers to paste up the rest of them."

Darkness was gathering.

Lucas was showing Catsfoot the loft in the *Gazette* office which he had converted into living accommodation.

"I've got a spare bunk," Lucas said. "I want you to stay here with me."

"Thanks. I'd like that."

Lucas, fetching blankets from a cupboard, said: "Bason's taking his time about putting up those posters. He should have . . ."

The thud of running feet floated into the loft.

Several pairs of feet. They were approaching the office. First they made a solid noise as they crossed the baked earth of the road. Then they echoed on the boardwalk.

There was a crash as the outer door burst open. And, at the same time, a whimpering cry.

In a couple of strides, Catsfoot reached the vertical ladder which descended into the printing department. Facing forward, he jumped the ten feet to the floor.

He saw Bason Thebes leaning over the sales counter. A Bowie knife was in his back. Blood was spreading through his greasy overalls. His desperate, agonised breathing blended briefly with the sound of men running across the main street, running away from the office.

CHAPTER FIVE

"Try to scare me!"

CATSFOOT gripped Bason's arm. He looked carefully at the Bowie knife. Before trying to remove it, he had to be sure that it had not penetrated a nerve-centre or blood vessel. If it had, it would have to remain where it was until the town doctor arrived.

"You're going to be all right, Bason," he said. "Just try to hold still."

With his free hand Catsfoot gently tore away the blood-soaked patch of clothing. The blade had entered just below the left shoulder blade, penetrating about half an inch. To a normal man, such a wound in this area would have been serious, even fatal. But Bason's accumulation of sheer fat had saved him. Finger pressure told Catsfoot that no great damage had been done.

Holding the knife at the point where it entered the flesh, he plucked it out.

Bason groaned, shivered, then fainted. At that moment, Lucas arrived. He was holding a medicine box.

"Take hold of his legs," Catsfoot said. "Get him on to the counter, face down."

When the unconscious Bason was lying on his stomach along the length of the sales counter, Catsfoot said: "It's not serious, but he'll need the doctor."

"I'll fetch him," Lucas said, turning to the door.

As Lucas went out, Catsfoot took a roll of bandage from the medicine box. After satisfying himself that the wound was clean, he pressed a thick pad of bandage over it to staunch the bleeding.

Bason's eyes flickered open. He stared in astonishment at the counter which was supporting him. Then he groaned. The sound was caused more by terror than by pain.

"It's all over," Catsfoot whispered to him and Bason seemed to relax immediately. "Nobody'll hurt you again—I'll see to that."

Bason said faintly: "They—they threw a knife at me!"

"I know. It hasn't done you much harm. You've lost some blood, that's all. Can you tell me what happened?"

For once in his life, Bason Thebes did not lie, boast or exaggerate. In faint words, he gave Catsfoot the story. . . .

Bason had felt resentful when he left the Gazette office with a dozen of the newly-printed posters folded under his arm, and carrying a bucket of paste and a brush. This extra work meant that he was already late for his supper and he would be a great deal later before he was finished. Grumbling to himself, he slapped a poster on the sprawling old hickory tree near the Gazette office. A few people gathered round as he did so and some of them asked him questions. Bason ignored them. He did not feel like providing extra information. He only felt like eating.

Next he stumped into Winchell Street, where he placed two more posters on the wall outside a carpenter's yard. As word spread, more people gathered to read them and to ask questions. Some of them followed him back into the main street. And it was then that Bason realised something which made him forget his delayed supper. Something which pleased him. It dawned on him that he was a centre of attraction. He was important. People were wanting to know things and he, Bason Thebes, was the man they were looking to for the answers.

At once, Bason's manner changed. His sullenly silent attitude vanished. So did his shambling walk. He became a brisk, decisive, grimly-smiling man of destiny. As he strode out with his posters and bucket of paste, he saw himself as a great leader who was being followed by an adoring band of lesser mortals.

Bason made for Buddy Lane's saloon, from which came a

faint buzz of talk and a clinking of glasses. A large notice board was mounted on the boardwalk rails outside the saloon. It was here, by tradition, that all public announcements were displayed. As Bason approached, it held a hand-scrawled notice about a dance in the mission hall which had been cancelled, and the date of the next cattle auction.

Bason stopped in front of it and set down his bucket. Solemnly, he opened a fresh poster as if he were an army commander unrolling a campaign map at the start of a crucial battle. He inwardly purred with satisfaction as a rapidly growing crowd pressed round him, reading the poster over his shoulders.

The questions came fast.

"Has Catsfoot got anythin' personal against Janamo?"

"How long will Catsfoot wait?"

"Supposin' Janamo don't hear about this?"

And, the most important question of all, was: "Why does Catsfoot wanta come here for a gunfight?"

To all of them Bason smiled mysteriously, while speaking vaguely about secret information which he could not discuss. He brushed a layer of paste on to the back of the poster. He began to smooth it on to the notice board. It was then that Buddy Lane came out of his saloon, followed by a group of customers.

Buddy pushed through the crowd. First he read the poster silently. Then he read it aloud and at the top of his voice. He made each word vibrate with indignation.

"There y'have it!" he shouted, when he had finished reading. "It ain't enough for Lucas to try to bait Janamo into comin' back here! Not near enough 'cause now we have this Catsfoot yip puttin' out a challenge to a gunfight with him! And where's the fight to be staged? It's to be right here, in *our* town! Who stands to get killed while them two are blastin' slugs at each other? We do! Who stands to be looted again when that gang come back? We do! I tell you, folks, Lucas and Catsfoot between 'em want to turn Meditation into some kinda battleground! Well, I say we've had enough. We've gotta do somethin' and do it darned quick!"

He was pleased by the rumble of support from most of the crowd. He knew that he must do something to erase the memory of his defeat by Catsfoot that afternoon. This was his chance. Buddy no longer felt so afraid of Catsfoot. In the past few hours his attitude towards the trail scout had dramatically changed. When Catsfoot had first arrived, Buddy had imagined that he was under the guns of a ruthless killer. Since then, having made discreet inquiries, he found that Catsfoot was no killer, if killing could be avoided, and was very far from being ruthless. He found that very reassuring.

Buddy, the sleek and plausible talking man, was expert at exploiting anything and everything—including the good-nature of others. No power on earth could have persuaded Buddy to resist a pitiless gunslinger such as Janamo. But, knowing now that it was safe to do so, he was eager to challenge the man who sought to rid Arizona of Janamo.

And at the back of Buddy's wretched little mind there was another and even more squalid idea. He had a hunch that, if the Mexican gunslinger did return to Meditation, he would show special mercy to the man who had led the resistance to Catsfoot. If other people were killed and looted while Buddy Lane was spared by a grateful Janamo, that would suit Buddy Lane very well. It would be good business.

Someone shouted to Buddy: "What *can* we do? Catsfoot's plenty tough and he knows what them guns of his are for!"

Buddy drew a fresh cheroot from his velveteen jacket. After lighting it, he said: "I ain't scared of Catsfoot! Just let him try to scare me!"

There was a murmur of surprise. This was unusual talk from the saloon keeper, who was certainly not noted for bravery.

Buddy continued: "But we're goin' to do this legal, folks! To-morrow we'll hold a town meetin' and we'll vote for Catsfoot to be put out of Meditation!"

With his last words, Buddy put out a hand, gripped a corner of the poster and ripped it down. Then he turned towards Bason Thebes. In the last few minutes Bason's dreams had faded. He no longer saw himself as a man of destiny. He felt a little afraid and very hungry. He decided to take the rest of the posters back to the *Gazette* office, explain what had happened to Lucas, then get home to his bowl of stew.

Bason was picking up his bucket when Buddy gripped the front of his overalls, twisting them in his hand.

"And where d'you think you're goin'?"

"B-back to Mister Lucas, sir."

"To tell him what I've been sayin', eh?"

"Y-yes . . . that's n-no . . ."

"You're a friend of Lucas and Catsfoot, aren't you?"

"I . . . I don't k-know!"

"Don't know who your friends are, eh? You work for 'em, don't you? And you still got a whole lot of them posters under y'arm. You know what I'm goin' to do with them posters you got there? I'm goin' to cut 'em and stuff the pieces down your overalls, so your friends Lucas and Catsfoot can spend the night tryin' to piece the bits together again."

There was an expectant titter.

Buddy wrenched the posters from Bason and asked: "Who's gotta a knife?"

A curved Bowie knife was handed to him. Buddy balanced it in his hand, looking at Bason.

"I've just had a better idea," Buddy said. "You can cut 'em up y'self, Bason!"

Bason stumbled back, quaking.

"I . . . I can't do that, sir!"

"You'd best take this knife and try!"

The blade was pushed under Bason's nose. Bason looked around him in gathering panic. He saw a circle of leering, hostile faces. As if magnetised, his eyes came back to the Bowie. And his nerve broke completely. Panic took over.

And at first panic was aided by luck . . .

Bason lowered his head and gathered himself for a charge through the crowd. While doing so, he forgot about the bucket in his right hand.

The bucket slapped against the lower part of Buddy's velveteen jacket. Paste cascaded out of it, some splattering over the saloon-keeper's elegant clothes, most of it hitting him on the side of his glossy black head.

Suddenly the saloon keeper was transformed from the central figure of a drama, to the central figure of a slapstick comedy. With paste flowing down him, he looked absurd. And the crowd laughed.

Nothing was more calculated to rouse Buddy to a crazed fury than being the object of laughter. For a few seconds he stood completely still, listening to the guffaws and feeling uncontrollable fury sweep through him. Fury against Bason in particular.

Bason, dropping the bucket, had burst through the circle. Moving at extraordinary speed for such a portly man, he was running along the centre of the street towards the distant *Gazette* office.

As if propelled from a catapult, Buddy started in pursuit. And the crowd followed, all of them now in a thoroughly amused mood, all fear and fury temporarily forgotten.

Buddy gained slowly on Bason. But it soon became clear that he would not catch him before he reached the newspaper office.

As Bason swung from the road on to the boardwalk, Buddy entirely lost his head. Without knowing what he was doing, he sought any means which might prevent Bason escaping.

The Bowie knife was still in his hand.

Buddy knew nothing about knife-throwing. In any case, a Bowie, being unevenly balanced, was unsuitable for throwing. It was designed as a hunting tool and for close-quarter fighting.

But, while running, Buddy threw the knife at Bason.

It was sheer chance that the aim was accurate, that it travelled in a fast spin, and that the blade entered Bason's back as he was about to burst through the door of the *Gazette* office.

Bason did not check his pace. The Bowie protruding from his overalls, he crashed into the building.

Now it was Buddy's turn to know panic. In a fraction of a second, as he saw what he had done, his madness left him. He knew only fear. He swerved away from the boardwalk and sped across the street. The others, almost equally afraid, followed him.

Lucas had put a mattress and blankets on the floor of his office. He and Catsfoot had shifted the desk aside to make room for an oil heater.

Bason lay there, fairly comfortable, while the bearded town doctor examined him.

"You've made a good job of stopping the bleeding," the doctor told Catsfoot. "He's not badly hurt, but he'll have to rest here for a few days until the wound heals."

Bason smiled up at them. He was recovering his nerve. He was beginning to feel something of a hero.

When the doctor left, Catsfoot went up to the loft without saying anything to Lucas. A few minutes later he returned wearing his fedora and his guns.

"Where are you goin'?" Lucas asked, his eyes on the .44 Dragoons and suspecting the answer.

"I'm going to see Buddy Lane. The two of us are going to do some straight talking. And while I'm about it, I'm going to settle things with any other folks who are thinking the same way as Buddy."

Lucas said awkwardly: "Buddy's a load of trouble—I'll not deny that. But the rest of the people are all right. It's just that they're scared stupid and a smooth talker like Buddy easily influences them."

"I'd already guessed that. But we've got a fight coming against Janamo and his riders. If we're going to win, we'll need the help of the folks. We can't fight the people of Meditation *and* Janamo. I'm going to try to make them see sense. And I'll try to make them see just what kind of wind-blown yip their Buddy Lane is."

Lucas said anxiously: "Wouldn't it be better to wait till tomorrow's town meeting and talk to them then? Like I said, there's not much wrong with the ordinary people here. But right now their thinking is lop-sided. They believe that you and I are bringing more danger to them. They are very afraid,

Catsfoot, and when even the most peaceful folks are scared they can become dangerous."

" The time to handle this is now. I've a hunch that Buddy will out-talk me easy if I wait for the town meeting."

Lucas said: " I'll come with you. I'll find someone to stay with Bason."

" Thanks for the offer," Catsfoot said, smiling, " but I want you to stay where you are."

" But I might be needed if . . ."

" No disrespect, but you do your fighting with a pen and you do it durned well. I do mine a different way. I'll handle this best if I don't have your safety to worry about."

Catsfoot tipped his fedora slightly forward over his eyes. He bent down to pat Bason on the shoulder. Then he glided out of the room.

There was a new kind of fear in Lucas's heart as he watched the tall, slender figure move past the printing machinery, past the sales counter which was still wet with blood, then out through the doorway.

Lucas went to the window. From there, he saw Catsfoot moving along the boardwalk. Moving so smoothly through the shadows and pools of light that he might have been a ghost.

Lucas waited until the silhouette of Catsfoot crossed the road and vanished in the direction of Buddy Lane's saloon.

CHAPTER SIX

The traitors

BUDDY LANE was feeling relieved. So were the others who had joined the pursuit of Bason. Word had quickly spread that Bason was not badly hurt.

"It was the fat yip's own fault!" Buddy announced in his saloon. "He tosses a bucket at me, so ain't I entitled to get mad?"

Seated on the edge of a small table, he looked searchingly at his customers. Some of them nodded approval. Others were not so sure and avoided his eye.

"Anyhow, nothin' has changed so far as Catsfoot's concerned," Buddy went on, smoothing the lapels of a grey silk jacket into which he had just changed. "At the meetin' to-morrow we tell that no-good cheapskate gunslinger we won't have him turnin' this town into no battleground! We . . ."

Buddy stopped abruptly. His eyes travelled to the swing doors.

It was impossible to say how long Catsfoot had been standing there. But certainly it was long enough for him to lean against the angle of the wall, to cross his long legs, to fold his arms over his chest. He was gazing across the saloon. Gazing directly at Buddy, a faint smile curving his lips.

A brief shuffle of uneasy movement came from the customers. The three barmen became tense.

For a mere moment, Buddy showed a flicker of fear. Then he remembered that Catsfoot was not another Janamo. He was, he reminded himself, safe enough. Catsfoot would not harm him.

"You sure have a nerve comin' into *my* saloon," Buddy said, getting to his feet and scowling. "I've a fair mind to have you tossed out!"

Catsfoot did not move. He remained completely relaxed as he said: "If anybody wants to try putting me out, I'm ready and waiting."

None of the customers moved. Buddy glared round the saloon.

"What are we waitin' for?" he asked. "There's plenty of us! Let's get busy!"

Still no reaction from the customers. Some were standing against the bar counter, others were sitting at tables. Each was waiting for someone else to give a lead. None fancied the prospect of being the first to tangle with this tall man in buckskins.

Catsfoot asked: "Why don't you show them how it should be done, Buddy?"

Buddy coloured. "I'm no fightin' man," he said.

Catsfoot nodded.

"I guess that's right. But it seems you're ready to get other folks to do your fighting for you. Or mebbe you like to wait till a man has his back to you, so you can throw a knife at him!"

Buddy's narrow face twitched. He smoothed his narrow moustache with the back of his hand, licked his dry lips with the tip of a very pink tongue.

"I've taken enough from you, Catsfoot," he said. "My barmen are goin' to bounce you out of my saloon!"

As he finished, Buddy nodded towards the three men behind the bar counter. They were burly men, all of them. Although there was seldom any trouble in the saloon, part of their job was to deal with it when it did come. They were not only professional barmen. They were also professional toughs.

The three groped under the counter. From a shelf there, each produced a stick. They were short sticks—no more than twelve inches from tip to tip. But they were as thick as a man's wrist. At one end they were bound with leather, to give a firm grip. At the other end they had been partly hollowed out and filled with lead. Even a moderate tap from one of those weighted batons could produce a serious injury.

Swinging their batons, the three men raised the hinged counter flap and passed through. Then they stood shoulder to shoulder, facing Catsfoot, who was about twenty feet from them. Their eyes were on his Dragoons and the sight of them was making them hesitate. Buddy noted the fact. He tried to re-assure them.

"Don't worry about them guns of his," he told his men. "If he uses 'em, he'll be a wanted man—wanted by the law! He's been told to get off my property and he's refused. That gives us a legal right to throw him out!"

Buddy was right—and Catsfoot knew it. Technically, he was a trespasser on the saloon keeper's property. To avoid trouble, he had only to leave. If he stayed and used his guns against men armed only with sticks, and they were killed or wounded, he would certainly be arrested as soon as the law was restored to this part of Arizona.

He could threaten the men with his guns, and hope that the sight of them would be enough to keep them off. But he knew that that was not likely to work. Not against these three, who were showing clear signs of accepting Buddy's reassurance. Their weighted batons raised, they moved slowly towards Cats-foot.

Catsfoot remained leaning against the wall. He did not un-cross his legs, did not unfold his arms.

Seven paces between the barmen and Catsfoot. . . .

Six paces. . . .

Five. . . .

The barmen stopped. They did so together and instinctively. This was something they could not have expected, which they did not understand. There was a chilling menace about this un-moving, unblinking man.

Buddy broke the tension. He gave a sudden jerk, as if waking from a nightmare. And in a hoarsely strained voice he shouted: "What are y'waitin' for? Don't be scared of his bluff! Take him. . . .!"

Sticks above their heads, the three started to rush the last few paces.

But they did not get far. They did not complete the short distance.

No one in the saloon could honestly claim that he saw Catsfoot draw his guns.

All that any of them clearly saw were two separate pictures of Catsfoot.

In the first, he was standing inert, his arms folded across his chest.

In the other, his hands were at waist level. The left hand was slightly extended, the right pulled back a little.

And a cocked .44 Dragoon was in each of them.

All of those who were watching wondered whether they had missed the draw because they had blinked their eyes at the vital moment. But none of them had blinked. They had been in the presence of the double-draw, as performed by one of the greatest experts on earth, and it had been far too fast for the eyes to follow.

But Catsfoot was not finished. Far from it. . . .

The saloon reverberated as the gun in Catsfoot's right hand was fired twice, the other once. Yet the three shots were discharged so quickly that, judged by sound alone, there might have been merely one. The separate bursts of yellow flame from the muzzles showed that a triple volley had been released. . . .

The clubs disintegrated.

The spinning, nickel-coated lead bullets, travelling at a velocity of fifteen hundred feet a second, sliced through the lead in the batons. The metal fillings expanded and burst out of the wood in a rain of small fragments which splattered harmlessly against the walls. And the men were left holding useless, splintered fragments which protruded scarcely more than an inch from their hands.

The barmen were not cowards. But this was more than the nerves of any ordinary mortals could be expected to stand.

One of them gaped in abject astonishment at Catsfoot, then at the tiny piece of wood which he was still holding. His lips began to tremble. Covering his face with an arm, he staggered to a chair. He was almost fainting as he flopped on to it.

The two others were made of slightly tougher material. They

shook their heads, as if seeking to clear them after the crash of gunfire. Then, trying to appear self-possessed but obviously scared to their foundations, they returned to their places behind the bar.

The customers were staring at Catsfoot as if emerging from a trance. Returning their gaze, Catsfoot felt a wave of hopeless depression. For he saw hatred as well as fear in their faces.

This was the result of the gun incident.

Catsfoot had not wanted to use his guns, but it had been forced on him. He had hoped to destroy Buddy's influence and gain general support for a stand against Janamo. Instead, because of the shooting, the men in the saloon saw him as much the same sort of gunslinger as the Mexican. Not so ruthless, perhaps. But basically the same. Which was exactly what Buddy Lane wanted. Buddy was winning this duel, Catsfoot admitted to himself.

Recovering his wits and realising that he had gained a huge advantage, Buddy opened a new attack.

" Now you've seen for y'selves what sorta yip Catsfoot is," he said to the customers. " What's the difference between him and Janamo? Has Catsfoot any more respect for property than the Mexican? Didn't Catsfoot refuse to move when I ordered him out of my saloon? And didn't he draw guns on my men— my *unarmed* men—when they tried to put him out?"

All of them were still too scared to do anything more than nod feeble approval. All except Abe Solomon, who had an independent mind and was shrewd enough to distrust most things about Buddy.

Abe had come into the saloon to relax after closing his mercantile store for the day. He was annoyed because nothing short of a hibernating tortoise could be expected to relax in this atmosphere. And because his Jewish commonsense, plus the evidence of his eyes, told him that it was absurd to present Catsfoot as a gun-happy killer. So Abe decided to speak up.

Rubbing the tip of his large nose, he said: " That sounds like a load of claptrap to me, Buddy."

All of them turned to where Abe was sitting alone in a corner.

The blunt and unexpected statement came as a shock. It even shook Buddy, but only for a moment.

"It might sound that way to you, Abe," Buddy retorted. "But the rest of us know all I've said is right."

Gesticulating with upturned palms, Abe said: "I don't want a gunfight here, and more'n the rest of you. I don't want to see Janamo and his mob back in town, neither. They're bad customers in my store! They take delivery, but they don't pay! All the same," he concluded, "I'm wonderin' if it wouldn't be best to face up to Janamo."

Suddenly, Catsfoot felt his depression vanish. Hope flared in its place. One man—an obviously responsible and cautious store-owner—was volunteering as an ally. He was tempted to move towards Abe and stand beside him, but he knew that, at this moment, it would be the wrong thing to do. Abe must be allowed to handle this himself. And he seemed well able to do so.

Buddy produced a sneering laugh.

"How the heck *can* we face up to him? Ain't he got a small army?"

"Sure—but we have enough men in this town to make a *big* army."

"That's crazy talk, Abe! It's bad enough havin' Catsfoot lookin' for a solo gunfight with Janamo. Now you're sayin' we should have a real war—Meditation against Janamo's gang! I'll tell you this, there wouldn't be much left of the town after the fightin's finished. There wouldn't be many folks left alive, neither!"

Abe smiled while giving Buddy a long, sideways look.

"Seems to me we might just as well organise to defend ourselves," he said, "seein' Janamo will be comin' back here anyway."

"What makes y'so sure he'll be back?"

"He'll hear about Catsfoot's challenge."

"We can stop them posters being scattered about the territory. And we can still stop Lucas makin' trouble in his paper."

"Mebbe you're right," Abe said. "But Janamo will still get

to know. Too many folks know about the challenge already.
Word's bound to reach him!"

Buddy jumped to his feet and brought a puny fist down on
to the table.

"Okay, but Janamo won't do nothin' to us if he gets here and
finds Catsfoot's gone! He'll be too durned anxious to get on
Catsfoot's trail to think about lootin' and killin' in Meditation
again!" Buddy paused, breathing heavily. He turned away from
Abe and pointed a quivering finger at Catsfoot. Then he
added: "To-morrow we have a town meetin' in the mission
hall! Then the folks'll decide to send you on y'way, 'cause we
don't want no part of you! It'll be the same for Ralph Lucas,
unless he acts sensible! A town meetin' is official and legal,
Catsfoot! If you're thinkin' you can ignore it, think again!
If you don't get out of here after the meetin', every grown man
in Meditation will have the right to shoot you on sight. They
can even shoot you in the back and it'll still be legal! You're
durned fast with your guns, but you wouldn't last five minutes
against the whole of this burgh!"

Someone stamped his feet to show approval. Others joined
him. Hand-clapping mingled with shouts of support. The
saloon was filled with a tornado of noise.

Abe Solomon tried to speak, but his words were inaudible and
he gave up the attempt.

Catsfoot watched them, his face suddenly drawn and weary,
his eyes heavy.

An empty beer glass flew towards him. It hit him on the
chest. But he did not move, did not seem even to have noticed it.

It was a signal for more missiles to be hurled at him. Most of
them missed. But a broken bottle struck the side of his chin,
opening a small cut. He seemed unaware of the wound and of
the blood dribbling on to his buckskin jacket.

At last, he turned his back on them and walked slowly through
the swing doors. The jeers of men who were afraid and secretly
ashamed, followed him into the night.

And at that same moment. less than fifty miles away, Janamo

and his killers were enjoying a new type of banditry. They had taken over a small wagon train, which was following the little-used trail between Phoenix and El Paso.

The operation had been almost too easy. . . .

The eight wagons had grouped into the usual defensive circle for the night. Just outside the perimeter two look-outs were posted. Inside the ring of wagons, the travellers were gathered round a tall fire, talking contentedly after a communal meal.

A shout from one of the look-outs sent the men rushing for their guns while women and children took cover inside the wagons. None of them doubted that, if this were a genuine alarm, it was because Apaches were on the prowl. They had had trouble with Apaches before, and had always beaten them off without much trouble.

The look-outs were the last to join the other men under the wagons. All of them listened to the steady beat of many cantering horses. Then, in the moonlight, a column of men became visible. Nothing much could be seen of them except that they were riding two abreast in military fashion and a man of enormous size was at their head.

" They look like soldiers," the elderly wagon master said, fingering his Hawkins Plains rifle.

" Sure do," the man next to him muttered.

" I'll give 'em a call. . . ."

The wagon master bellowed a challenge. At once, the column came to a halt. The giant of a man who was leading them called back : " This is D Troop, the Seventh U.S. Cavalry. I'm Major John Jones and I'm in command. Who are you?"

The wagon master chuckled.

" Just a few settlers and traders makin' for El Paso! We sure would be glad to have you camp by us to-night. Haven't seen many fresh faces lately."

" Me and m'men would be glad to join you," the giant said. He raised an arm, and the column resumed its approach.

Chattering excitedly, the women and children were emerging. The men were gathering outside the circle to greet the visitors.

But one man among them looked puzzled. Scratching his head, he moved through the shadows to the wagon master and said: " Somethin' ain't right here."

" What ain't right?"

" I've served a couple of years in the cavalry. That's long enough to know there ain't never less than sixty men in a troop, and sometimes a hundred. There don't seem to be more than about twenty in that column."

The veteran wagon master snorted his impatience.

" Ain't a cavalry troop entitled to be short of men?"

" Mebbe, but there's somethin' else. That officer says he's a major. But a troop's always commanded by a captain! I've never heard of a major in charge of only twenty men! And the Seventh Cavalry's never been nowhere near these parts. It operates in the Dakotas, Wyoming and Montana. But this hombre says they're part of the Seventh!"

Suddenly the wagon master became uneasy. His doubts were converted into certainty when a settler shouted wildly: " *They* ain't soldiers! They ain't in uniform!"

But the warning came much too late. It came when the front of the column was a mere twenty yards away. A few of the men, including the wagon master, tried to get back to their defence positions. They scarcely had time to move a single step before they found themselves surrounded by the horsemen, each of whom was levelling a double-action Remington rimfire gun at them.

And that was the beginning of the enjoyable experience for Janamo and his men.

One of the wagons was owned by a silversmith who had intended opening a business in El Paso. His entire working capital, nearly ten thousand dollars, was found in his cash box. It was put in Janamo's saddlebag, to be shared out later.

The other travellers were also swiftly relieved of their cash. None of them had nearly so much as the silversmith, but the total came to a useful sum.

The looting over, the riders gathered comfortably round the fire, watching and talking while a meal was prepared for them.

They had just finished eating when news from Meditation reached Janamo.

It came by chance. And it was brought by a good-natured and comparatively harmless villain who called himself Doc Parker.

Doc Parker—who, in fact, was no doctor at all—drove slowly along the trail in a battered gig which was drawn by a wind-blown cayuse. He had intended to camp several miles farther back. But he had been attracted by the sight of the fire reflecting in the night sky. He guessed that this might be a wagon train. Wagon trains often provided willing customers for the concoctions which he sold as medicines.

As he neared the wagons, he stopped for a few minutes to brush down his shiny frock coat, to place a frayed top hat on his head and to comb his small and sharply pointed black beard. Appearance counted for a lot in his trade.

Doc Parker was not at all disturbed when two men with Remingtons came out of the gloom. He took them to be the usual wagon train guard. Without speaking, the men led him and his gig into the middle of the circle.

Pleased to see an audience waiting for him, Doc Parker stood upright in his gig. He made a sweeping bow, describing a semicircle with his top hat.

" I come to you," he announced, " to cure your ills. I'm Doc Parker, lately private physician to the Presidents of the United States. Tell me what ails you and I will gladly sell you the remedy."

There was a long silence while more than twenty pairs of eyes fixed upon him. And from the wagons, the faces of the looted and captive travellers appeared. Doc Parker began to feel uneasy. Then Janamo, his huge length sprawling on the ground, said: " Carry on with the sales talk, Doc. You're doin' fine!"

Doc Parker opened a bulging leather case. From out of it he took a bottle of evil-looking purple liquid.

" Do you suffer from headaches?" he asked. " If so, this remarkable potion, prepared from a secret formula, will cure them. It will also cure poor eyesight, deafness, rheumatism and flat feet. . . ."

He prattled on. Doc Parker was one of many hundreds of quacks in the West who made a living out of public gullibility. A few of them sold medicines which were capable of causing real harm. But most of them merely retailed coloured, flavoured water, and pills which consisted of bread pellets encased in sugar. Doc Parker was one of the majority—his offerings were both harmless and useless.

Doc Parker was describing a treatment for ingrowing toenails when Janamo gave a loud yawn and asked: "Why don't y'peddle that stuff to townsfolk? I know a burgh near here that's just had a tough time. I guess they can use plenty of medicine. A place called Meditation."

On hearing the name, Doc Parker shrugged and looked sad.

"I was going to call at Meditation," he said. "But I changed my mind."

"Why?" Janamo asked without much interest.

"I met a copper miner who needed treatment for a cough. He told me that there could be a gunfight any time now in Meditation. I don't like fighting. A man can get hurt when . . ."

Raising himself on one elbow and suddenly alert, Janamo asked: "Who's gunnin' for who? Did you hear that?"

"Yep," Doc Parker said innocently. "Catsfoot, the trail scout, is in Meditation. He's waiting to nail a Mexican gunslinger called Janamo."

"Is that so," Janamo said, very softly.

"Sure is. I've heard plenty about Catsfoot while moving about. Folks do say he's real fast with his guns."

"And what do they say about Janamo?" Janamo asked.

"He's supposed to be plenty fast, too. I figure there'd be nothing between those two, if they ever do meet. Most likely, they'd nail each other. But, of course, I'd like to see Catsfoot come off best."

"You would, uh? Why?"

"Because Catsfoot's no killer. He's a fine man, there's no doubt about that."

"What's wrong with Janamo?"

"Janamo! Heck, you must have heard about that Mexie and his gang!"

"Don't think I have. You tell me."

"Well, Janamo ain't like a human being at all. They say he's more like one of those gruntin' gorillas that live in Africa. Huge, he is. He . . ."

"Would he be about my size?" Janamo asked, getting to his feet.

"Yep, I guess he would . . ."

The sentence faded and perished at the back of Doc Parker's throat. His eyes dilated like those of a fish as they took in the massive structure of Janamo.

"Can he use a gun like this . . .?"

A crash came from a gun which had suddenly appeared in Janamo's right hand. Doc Parker's top hat floated high into the night air.

Doc Parker was still holding the bottle of purple medicine. Without appearing to take aim, Janamo blasted it out of his hand with his second shot.

A frightened horse whinnied. From inside one of the wagons a woman screamed.

Doc Parker, on the point of collapse, turned to jump from his gig. But he froze still when Janamo bellowed: "Hold still, Doc! I figure you can use a shave. . . ."

The pill peddler felt a momentary draught under his chin. He raised a shaking hand, then gave an incredulous bleat. His newly-combed, smartly pointed black beard had vanished. In its place he could feel only an untidy tuft of short hair. Yet the bullet had not touched his skin.

And that marked the end of Doc Parker's endurance. It also marked the end of his life. He fainted and was falling forward, already mercifully unconscious, when one of Janamo's rimfire bullets bored through his chest.

Janamo wiped sweat from his fleshy face. He extracted four empty cartridge cases from his double-action Remington, replaced them with new shells.

His men were gathering round him. He turned to them.

" So Catsfoot wants a fight, uh?" he said almost dreamily, as if tasting and enjoying each word. " I won't disappoint him. And after I've settled with Catsfoot, we'll all get to work on Meditation . . . we'll wipe out that burgh . . . we'll burn it to cinders . . . then mebbe folks in this territory will know it don't pay to challenge Janamo. . . ."

CHAPTER SEVEN

From Janamo . . .

CATSFOOT did not go straight back to the *Gazette* office after leaving the saloon. Instead, he walked slowly south along the main street. He passed Abe Solomon's shuttered store, in front of which a stray dog was prowling. He passed Pat O'Toole's Luxury Rooming House, where Pat himself was lounging in the doorway with a group of copper miners. All of them stared at Catsfoot coldly. One of them shouted something after him. Catsfoot did not catch the words, but he knew that they were not complimentary.

He was glad when the town was behind him.

To his left, a hundred yards from the trail, he saw a cluster of rocks gleaming under the moon. He made for them because they looked peaceful and secure. He needed such a place. A place where he could be alone and think.

There was a shallow opening in the side of one of the rocks which offered protection against winds from the Yuma Desert. Those winds, scorching during the day, were bitterly cold at night. Catsfoot sat in the opening. He turned up the collar of his buckskin jacket and while doing so was surprised to feel dried blood on his face. Then he remembered the broken bottle which had been thrown at him. . . .

For half an hour he remained there, gazing at the sweep of the dark sky, hearing the moan of the wind in the sagebrush. His heart had never before been so heavy, nor his mind so troubled.

When he got to his feet and began walking back into town, he had reached a vital decision.

Bason Thebes was sleeping peacefully in Lucas's office. Catsfoot glanced at him, then mounted the vertical ladder into the converted loft.

He was surprised to find Lucas not only awake, but fully dressed. Even more surprising, Abe Solomon was sitting opposite Lucas, in an easy-chair.

Both men looked relieved as Catsfoot entered.

"We've been worried about you," Lucas said. "Abe says you left the saloon a long while back."

Catsfoot tossed his fedora on to his bunk. He unbuckled his gun belt and draped it over a wall hook. Then he sank back into Lucas's settee.

"I wanted to sort something out in my mind," he said.

Abe directed his quizzical sideways look at Catsfoot.

"What was it?" he asked.

"I had to figure out what's best for this town—whether I ought to stay and fight, no matter what happens, or whether I'd better quit."

"And what have you decided, Catsfoot?"

"I've decided to quit."

He made the statement flatly, tonelessly. Abe began furiously to rub his prominent nose. Lucas swung his head round and almost glared at Catsfoot.

"You can't do that!" Lucas snapped.

"I can and I will! I can only help to save places like Meditation from Janamo if they want to be helped. I can do nothing if the ordinary folks are against me."

Abe cleared his throat and fluttered his hands.

"What makes you so sure the ordinary folks *are* against you?" he asked.

Catsfoot gave a tired smile.

"You were at the saloon to-night. You saw what happened. In a few hours they'll hold their town meeting and order me out. They've made their feelings plain enough."

Abe said: "They could be just scared, Catsfoot! I figure that deep in their hearts most of 'em know you're right."

"What difference does it make what's in their hearts, Abe? It's what they're doing that matters." He hesitated, then added huskily: "They hate me, they throw glasses and bottles at me, they shout insults at me! This is something that's never happened to me before. I've never been hated by ordinary decent folk!"

"So you admit they're decent folk," Abe said quietly. "You admit that, even when they're doin' all this to you?"

"Of course I do. There's nothing bad about them—except mebbe for one or two like Buddy Lane. It's just that they've got things all wrong. This town's had it too soft, I guess, and when things turn tough they look for the easy way out."

Abe pulled out a fob watch, looked at it, then said: "If you quit, Catsfoot, this town will die! It'll die because the man who can save it has backed out just when he's needed most. There isn't a lot of time left. It'll soon be daylight and I'll have to go. Before I leave, I hope you'll tell me you've changed y'mind."

His momentary annoyance fading, Catsfoot said: "I'm grateful for the way you spoke up for me in the saloon, Abe. If the town had a few more people like you and Ralph Lucas, things would've turned out different. But my mind hasn't changed. I'm going to have a few hours sleep. Then I'm riding out of town before they hold their meeting."

Lucas suddenly stood up. There was a strange intensity about him as he faced Catsfoot.

"Before you go, I want you to let me have one of your guns," he said.

Catsfoot blinked at him, as if not sure that he had heard rightly.

"You—you want me to give you a gun!"

"That's what I said."

"What will you be doing with a gun?"

"I'm going to have it in my hand when Janamo returns to this town! I'm going to try to kill Janamo!"

Catsfoot was silent for a time, staring blankly at Lucas. Then he gave a deep sigh.

"That's just about the craziest talk I've ever heard," he said.

"Crazy or not, *someone's* got to face up to that gunslinger! I've already done it once—and I was unarmed that time. I guess I might do better with a Colt to help out!"

Speaking slowly, so that every word would take effect, Catsfoot said: "You'd have no chance at all of harming Janamo! You wouldn't even worry him if you pressed a gun in his stomach while he had his hands in his pockets! So be sensible! Forget that stupid talk!"

Lucas shook his head.

"I'm not all that stupid, Catsfoot. I know I won't have any sort of chance. But it's the example that'll count. I'm hoping that if the people see just one man standing up to Janamo, it'll encourage them to fight! I think that's something worth dying for. So let me have a gun before you quit!"

Abe moved towards Lucas and stood beside him.

"You won't be alone," he said. "It so happens I own a gun. We'll face it together when Janamo arrives. Mebbe between us we'll nail him—miracles do sometimes happen!"

Catsfoot looked from one to the other. He saw beyond all doubt that this was no mere bravado. Both the editor and the Jewish storekeeper were completely genuine in their determination to shoot it out with the Mexican. He made a new decision. He had no choice.

Catsfoot got off the settee and said: "I'm not giving away a gun. I'm going to need both of them. No matter what they decide at the meeting, I'm going to stay in town. And when Janamo arrives, *I'll* be the one who's waiting for him. . . .!"

The mission hall was packed, stifling hot, seething with excitement. Some of the townsfolk had even climbed on to the high roof rafters.

There were a few faint hisses when Catsfoot arrived followed by Lucas and Abe Solomon. They managed to find a place against a wall.

A few minutes later, a burst of applause greeted Buddy Lane. Space was willingly made for him as he strutted importantly towards the platform, a cheroot in the long holder clenched between his teeth. O'Toole and four other members of the Town Committee were with him.

Buddy did not waste time. As soon as he had mounted the platform, he raised his hands for silence.

" Folks," he said, " we're here to decide whether one man's to be allowed to turn Meditation into a battleground! And if another man—our local newspaper editor—is to be allowed to play along with him! A few weeks ago Janamo was here and we all suffered because of it. One of our friends lost his life. It was a relief to all of us when the Mexicans left. Now Catsfoot and Lucas aim to bring Janamo back to Meditation—they *want* a gunfight with him right here. . . ."

Skilfully, Buddy developed his familiar argument. His points were punctuated by frequent applause. He finished by saying: " So we put it to a vote. Do we order Catsfoot to clear out of Meditation right away? And do we tell Lucas to lay off goadin' Janamo, or we'll stop him printin' his paper? All those who agree raise their hands. . . ."

A great forest of hands went up. But most of them wavered and descended when it was seen that Catsfoot was pushing and elbowing his way towards the platform. Buddy watched him with faint anxiety.

" You can't come up here!" he said. " The platform's for the Town Committee only!"

But the warning was useless. Catsfoot arrived with a smooth handspring. He was speaking partly to Buddy and partly to the crowd as he said: " You've taken your vote! You've decided that I've got to go! But you've done it without hearing what I've got to say! Plenty's been said against me, but I haven't had a chance to reply! Is this supposed to be justice? Is this how you always run this town?"

The words got home to at least some of the audience—the fact was revealed by faces which had become suddenly thoughtful.

But Buddy was not disturbed. He smiled blandly.

" You ain't got no right to speak at a town meeting," he said, " because you don't belong to Meditation. That's one of our local laws! It's a town ordinance!"

" Okay, mebbe that's right," Catsfoot admitted. " But what about Ralph Lucas?"

Buddy asked cautiously: "Lucas? Don't know what y'mean."

"*He* belongs to Meditation, doesn't he?"

"Sure, but . . ."

"And he's been warned by this meeting. Warned to watch what he writes in his paper—hasn't he?"

"Yep. . . ."

"Then why wasn't he allowed to speak? Tell me that!"

Buddy's bland smile had vanished. The hall was silent, expectantly awaiting his answer.

Buddy knew that he was in a trap of his own making. Over-anxious to have the vote taken, he had ignored Lucas's right to be heard in his own defence. He played for time. He squeezed the cheroot out of its long holder and carefully stood on it. Then, forced to say something, he produced only hesitant verbal fluff.

"I gotta say, folks, that . . . well, we gotta understand this is a special kind of meetin' because . . . because everythin' is special so this is . . ."

That was as far as he got.

He stopped talking when he became aware of a weird tension.

A Mexican half-breed ambled in. They all recognised him. One of Janamo's men. A man whose skin was the colour of saddle-leather, who was showing very white teeth in a cruel parody of a smile.

He was very sure of himself as, hands on his hips, he halted just inside the hall and looked over the massed heads towards the platform.

"Catsfoot here?" he asked.

"I'm Catsfoot." Catsfoot answered without moving.

"I gotta message for you. It's from Janamo."

"I'm listening."

"Janamo'll meet you to-day. He says for you to be in the main street at high noon, ready to make your play. That's the message."

Quietly, Catsfoot said: "Tell Janamo I'll be there."

The half-breed turned and was about to leave.

But Buddy Lane stopped him.

Buddy had been watching and listening while his face pulsated with fear. Now, his eyes wild, he rushed to the edge of the platform, stretching out an imploring arm.

" Stop ! " It was almost a scream.

The half-breed looked at Buddy with flinty amusement, remembering the saloon keeper who had snivelled and grovelled to them during their occupation of the town.

" Yeah? What does the pot-boy want?" he asked.

Buddy was beyond even hearing the insult.

" There's no need for Janamo to come into Meditation ! " Buddy gabbled wildly. " We've just had an official town meetin' and we've ordered Catsfoot outa town. He'll be goin' right now—we'll see to that ! We don't want no part of Catsfoot, don't like him no more than Janamo does ! "

" That so?" the half-breed asked, showing more of his teeth.

" Yep ! In fact we'll do more to help Janamo ! We all want to help him ! So y'can take Catsfoot with you right now ! Y'can take Catsfoot to Janamo personal—how's that?"

" Nice of you to think that way. But Janamo says to meet Catsfoot right here at high noon, and that's the way it's goin' to be. If he ain't in the main street, it'll go mighty rough on all of you ! "

The half-breed looked slowly round the hall. Then he moved smilingly out.

Buddy watched him go and a shiver, like that of a man in a fever, possessed his puny frame. He turned to Catsfoot, seemed about to plead with him, changed his mind and took a running jump from the platform.

The jump was so quick, so unexpected, that those packed immediately below had no chance to squeeze out of the way. Buddy crashed on to them, then fell between several reeling men. But he was back on his feet at once. And he was frantically thrusting and elbowing his way towards the door. It took him a full minute to get out of the hall and stand panting on the boardwalk. He was in time to glimpse the half-breed as he vanished round a slight bend near the southern end of the street.

Sweat streaming from his face, he sped towards his saloon, watched by gaping townsfolk.

Buddy did not enter his saloon. Instead, he skirted round the side of the building and clattered into a small paved yard where there was a water pump, a trough, and a stable.

Bursting into the stable, he threw saddle and bridle on to his horse. Buddy was not a riding man. For days on end, he would scarcely put a head out of his saloon. As a result, his dapple-grey mare was fat and wheezy through lack of exercise. It whinnied with disgust as Buddy climbed awkwardly on to its back and smote its quarters with a crop.

Despite Buddy's urgings, the animal could achieve little more than a gentle canter down the main street in pursuit of the half-breed.

By this time, most of Meditation was watching, including those who had packed into the Mission Hall.

It happened that the half-breed was in no hurry. Janamo and the rest of the men were resting in a small canyon, just north of the trail and less than five miles out of town. That, and the fact that he had quickly found Catsfoot, meant that he could return at a walking pace. They had been riding hard all night from the place where they had left the wagon train. So it was natural to want to take it easy.

That was why Buddy managed to catch up with the half-breed after covering three miles.

Hearing his approach, the half-breed reined in and waited. Recognising Buddy, he took his hand away from the butt of his Remington.

"I did all my talkin' in town," he said. "It ain't no use followin' me around."

Buddy gasped: "I gotta talk to Janamo!"

"You'll see him at high noon. That's not much more'n an hour from now. Mebbe he'll let you talk to him then, if you ask him nice."

"It's urgent business—can't wait!"

"Ain't I already told you he's comin' into Meditation to fix Catsfoot? You won't talk him out of doin' that, so you . . ."

"That's not what I want to see him about!"

"What, then?"

"It's . . . it's kinda confidential."

The half-breed hesitated. He decided that there could be no harm in taking the saloon keeper to Janamo. Whatever he had to say could be important.

"Okay," the half-breed said, flashing his teeth, "I'll take you to Janamo. . . ."

Janamo gnawed at a leg of newly-fried chicken. Hot grease dribbled down his bristly chin and splashed on to a new linen shirt which was part of the booty from the wagon train.

"Talk, talk fast, and you'd best talk good!" he said.

Buddy almost shuddered. The canyon was small in length, but impressive in height. It gave him an uncomfortable feeling of being held captive. He felt a twinge of doubt about whether he should have come here.

"When y'were in Meditation, I always did m'best to string along with you," Buddy said in tones which were partly a whine and partly a piece of self-congratulation. "I never tried to hide anything from you, like a lot of other folks did. I handed over all you wanted without no trouble."

Janamo was not even looking at him—he was concentrating on the chicken as he said: "Sure, y'did all right, Buddy. We didn't have trouble from you."

Buddy felt his heart lift. Encouraged, he said: "Thanks, Janamo. I sure am glad you noticed how I tried to help. Mebbe you've heard how I've tried to run Catsfoot out of town on account of what he's been sayin' about you. I've been workin' on the newspaper editor, too. I stood by you, even after you left Meditation, Janamo. I'd never hear anyone say anythin' against you."

"That's kinda nice to know," Janamo said quietly. "I like to have friends—good friends like you, Buddy. Now tell me why you've come out here."

"I . . . well, y'see, I'd sure be glad if you'd leave me and my saloon alone when you come into Meditation to-day. Tell your boys not to rough me up none, and not to loot my saloon no more. I guess some of the others in town deserve all you're goin' to give 'em, Janamo! But I ain't like them! Like you say, I'm a friend of yours!"

"Y'just want to be left alone, uh? You don't want to be hurt none, you don't want us to take no more of your property—that right?"

"Yep—on account of the way I've always spoke up for you!"

Janamo bent down, picked a twig from the ground. He sharpened it with a short belt knife, then used it to dislodge chicken from between his teeth. Buddy waited respectfully.

When Janamo had finished, he said: "That's nice clothin' y'got on, Buddy."

Buddy glanced down at his lavender-blue suit over a hand-embroidered waistcoat. It was a little rumpled as a result of the mission hall meeting, but it was still unusual and impressive.

"Thanks, Janamo," Buddy said, feeling that he was making good progress with the Mexican. "I kinda like it, too. I got it . . ."

Janamo's knife flashed out. Flashed towards Buddy. But it did not touch his flesh. It in no way harmed him. It only harmed his clothes.

First, the blade ripped up the front of the splendid waistcoat. Then, with a flick of his wrist, Janamo sliced down the centre of Buddy's jacket. Buddy gazed aghast at the garments which were hanging from him like rags. Some of Janamo's men, who were rubbing down their horses, stopped to watch and laugh.

"Why . . . why did you do that?" Buddy asked after a long struggle to control his voice.

"Because you're a little runt, Buddy, and I don't like you no more'n I like anybody from Meditation!"

Buddy became pale and another fit of trembling began.

"Y'not goin' to kill me! I ain't done . . ."

"We won't kill you, Buddy," Janamo said gently. "We're not goin' to harm a hair of y'head. We're goin' to send you right back to Meditation and you're goin' to have new clothes to go in. You're goin' to wear a horse-blanket!"

" Horse-blanket! You'd put me in one of . . ."

" That's right, Buddy. You can't go back to town wearin'
that torn-up suit, can you? Take it off! Trousers, jacket, shirt
—everythin' you've got on. You've got one minute, or I'll
change m'mind about not hurtin' you!"

Buddy knew that further protest would not only be useless—
it would also be dangerous. Palpitating, he took off his clothes.
As he finished, one of the gang handed a horse-blanket to
Janamo. Janamo tossed it to Buddy.

" Put it on!" he ordered.

Trembling, Buddy draped the horse-blanket round his small,
skinny body. Loud laughter echoed through the canyon. Even
Janamo smiled.

" Tie it up," Janamo said.

With fumbling fingers, Buddy knots the tapes which were intended to secure the blanket under a horse's belly.

" Now y'can ride back to Meditation," Janamo said, pointing
to Buddy's fat mare. " And don't take too long gettin' there.
We'll be followin' soon. If we find you still on the trail, I'll
empty a slug into you!"

Holding the blanket up with one hand, Buddy climbed into
the saddle, listening to the laughter. He had ceased to tremble
as he headed back to town. And on his normally crafty face
there was dawning of a new and, as yet indefinable expression.

The eight covered wagons had abandoned the Phoenix-El
Paso Trail. They were moving fast over rough country—so fast
that wheels and axles would soon have snapped had they been
fully loaded. But the wagons were lightly laden. The looting
had seen to that. Janamo and his men had had no use for the
heavier articles with which the travellers had hoped to equip
their new homes—articles such as furniture. But these they had
burnt before the eyes of their owners as a final gesture before
leaving for Meditation. Now none of the wagons carried much
more than a handful of people.

The wagons, too, were making for Meditation. The decision

to go there had been reached very soon after the looters had had left them.

But they were taking a circuitous route, hoping to keep well out of the way of the gang. And hoping that, by some miracle, they would still arrive in Meditation before Janamo.

Janamo and his men were preparing for the short ride into Meditation. Guns were being checked, bridles and girth straps were being tightened. In a few minutes, when Janamo gave the word of command, they would mount. They would form into a perfect double file. And, at another command, they would move out of the canyon, keeping a column formation which would not discredit the United States Cavalry.

Watching them, Janamo felt pleased. These men of his had become the perfect instruments of terror. He, Janamo, had made them that way. He had taken the raw material of mere brutality and out of it he had moulded his own army. Superbly efficient, blindly obedient, utterly ruthless.

He told himself that his decision to destroy Meditation by fire would prove a wise one. When word of it reached other towns, there would be even less resistance to him than now. There would be even more willing co-operation from whelps like Buddy Lane.

But there had been a moment of indecision before he decided to burn the town. The question which had made him pause was: would it result in United States soldiers being sent against him? He had decided that there was little risk of that. The soldiers were stretched to near the limit guarding the new railroad against the Apaches. And those same Apaches were receiving plenty of encouragement from Janamo to keep up the pressure. In the last few weeks he had supplied guns and ammunition to them in plenty—all of it surplus loot from towns he had occupied. The Apaches were well satisfied with the deal. So was Janamo.

But, before the town was burnt, there was the gunfight with this Catsfoot. . . .

Over the years, he had heard many fragments of information concerning Catsfoot. Most of it was about how the trail scout had brought wagon trains through Indian territory and it had not interested him at all. But other items had stuck in his mind. And they had rankled, although he would never admit it to anyone except himself. Those items were about the trail scout's gunplay. It was supposed to be good. Janamo, with the generosity of a man who knows he is unbeatable, was prepared to accept that Catsfoot might even prove his fastest enemy yet. But he did not doubt that he would nail Catsfoot easily enough. There had been other stories about other fast guns. Janamo had met them. And only Janamo had walked away from those meetings.

As he mused, Janamo's eyes chanced to rest on the half-breed. He nodded his head. The half-breed gave up adjusting a stirrup leather and approached Janamo at a trot.

" Tell me about Catsfoot," Janamo said. " What kinda man is he?"

The half-breed looked surprised, then uncertain.

" I only saw him for mebbe three minutes, Janamo, in this big meetin' place."

" All right, so you only saw him for three minutes. Y'still *saw* him, didn't you? What does he look like?"

The half-breed said: " He's tall but he ain't so broad. He's in buckskins. Wears his hair kinda long to his shoulders. It's fair hair. . . ."

He finished lamely, his descriptive powers exhausted.

" Those guns of his," Janamo asked slowly, " was he wearin' 'em when y'saw him?"

" Sure was, Janamo."

" Does he carry 'em good?"

The half-breed answered with sudden urgency: " He looks like he knows what they're for! He never said nothin' much while I was there, but he gave me the idea he's . . . well, he's dangerous! Real dangerous! And real fast, too! Y'can see it in his body and his face. But in his face, mostly, if y'know what I mean."

Janamo's thoughts were drifting as he gave the half-breed a nod of dismissal. . . .

Drifting, yet fastening on to the fact that even one of his own men had been impressed by Catsfoot. So it seemed as if Catsfoot might have something, Janamo decided. That suited him. It'd make a change to come against some real opposition. He had often wondered what it must feel like to know that there was going to be no more than a fraction of a second between yourself and the other man.

This was something he couldn't imagine happening to *him*! For Janamo, gunfights were always routine, pallid affairs. Mere executions. And he was satisfied that they would always be so.

What else could be expected? Had he not trained to be the supreme gunfighter since he was a mere child? Since the days he had accompanied his father in service with a brigand gang in the Sierra Madre.

Hours every day it had been, practising the draw from just one position. And not just for a few days. Oh, no! That was not how Janamo had prepared himself. It had been week after week, month after month. Until arm and body ached and he felt sick at the sight of his gun. But he had kept going because this was the way, the only way, to become the undisputed master.

He wanted to see fear in men's eyes when he held out his hand and said: " My name's Janamo?"

Months of doing nothing else than maybe work on the Flat Draw. The draw which began and ended while standing still and facing front. It was the easiest of the lot, which meant it was just a bit less difficult than the five other basic positions from which a gun could be drawn.

After the Flat Draw, five or six months on the Falling Whip. More months on the Swivel Shift. And at the end of, say, three years, you were still no more than ordinarily good when placed against the top gunslingers.

His breakthrough had come after seven years, when he was eighteen. It happened in a cantina in Jalapa, capital of the Mexican province of Veracruz. Janamo had quarrelled with a much older man who was reputed to be the province's top gunfighter. Janamo recalled his surprise when he saw the other man drop, his gun scarcely out of its holster. Then his pleasure. It was then he realised that the long years were paying off. He was fast—real fast. People were beginning to talk about him. Because of his physique as well as his gun, they were careful not to annoy him.

But he had not stopped there. No relaxation. Practice for hours every day.

At the age of twenty he had felt confident enough to challenge the leader of his brigand gang. Janamo was acclaimed the new leader as the old one was carried away. And it was out of this gang that he had, over the years, created *his* riders.

So here he was, capable of nailing anything on two feet, or four. Supreme among . . .

Janamo saw that his men were ready. They were standing by their horses, looking curiously at him and awaiting the order to mount.

He boomed out a command. Twenty-two men swung into their saddles. At his leisure, Janamo mounted. And he led his riders out of the canyon, towards the trail for Meditation.

He was feeling much less happy now. Something to do with Catsfoot was annoying him. No, not Catsfoot's guns this time. But something else which he could not define.

They had covered half the distance to Meditation when he realised what it was.

He, Janamo, was doing exactly what Catsfoot wanted him to do! Catsfoot had arrived in Meditation and said, in effect, " I want Janamo to come to me."

And Janamo was doing just that!

Janamo muttered to himself: " I won't make it easy for him. . . . . I'll fix Catsfoot so he takes a long time to die. . . ."

CHAPTER EIGHT

Guns at noon

CATSFOOT finished cleaning and oiling his Colt Dragoons. He laid them on a table in the living quarters above the *Gazette* office. Glancing at the wall clock, he thought:, " Twenty minutes after eleven . . . forty minutes left. . . ."

Then another thought ran through his brain. It was one which he had tried to suppress, but it kept reappearing.

" Mebbe I'll be dead . . . forty minutes from now. . . ."

He had to admit to himself that this fight with Janamo was different to anything that had happened to him before. His usual self-confidence was not there. The idea kept percolating that maybe he was not so fast as Janamo. The idea that, in a mere forty minutes, amid a brevity of agony before the final blackness, he would know that at last he had met his master.

What was it the marshal had said in Tucson?

Yes, that lawman's words came back . . .

" It doesn't matter how fast you are, there's always another gun, waitin' somewhere, that's faster."

That had been his warning. A warning from a wise and experienced man.

Catsfoot wondered about the dryness at the back of his throat, the flutterings in his stomach. Was it just ordinary tension? It couldn't be, because he'd never felt like this before. So most likely it was a foreboding of disaster. A warning that he must be ready for the moment of absolute defeat. . . .

He forced the thought out of his mind by concentrating on his immediate task.

Out of his jacket he took a heavy carton made of waxed cardboard, which he had bought just before leaving Tucson. It contained thirty-six Graydon and Haynes .44 cartridges. He had been lucky to get them. Very expensive and double-checked at every stage of manufacture, Graydon and Haynes ammunition was not much seen in the New territories. Catsfoot thought that if it had always been available, he would probably never have needed to master the difficult technique of the double-draw. He used two guns, and always fired two shots together, as a precaution against a bad cartridge. Many a man had won on the draw and pressed the trigger first, only to be killed because of a misfire.

It was the knowledge that Janamo, along with all his men, used the new double-action Remington rimfires which decided Catsfoot to make certain changes to his cartridges. The Remington was a slightly heavier calibre gun than the Dragoon, with a longer range and a flatter trajectory. It was also commonly supposed to be capable of faster shooting than any other gun because of its double-action. But Catsfoot was not so sure of this. Shooting off bullets fast was no advantage unless they were aimed accurately. He suspected that cocking a gun by squeezing the trigger must upset the aim because the poundage needed to pull the trigger back was constantly changing—two pounds pressure was all that was needed at the beginning, in the case of the Remington, but it rose to five pounds at the moment before the hammer fell. And the trigger itself had to travel twice as far as any ordinary single-action.

But Catsfoot's immediate concern was to increase the flat-trajectory range of his Dragoons, so that they matched that of Janamo's Remington.

He gripped a cartridge between two pairs of pincers which he had borrowed from the printing department. He was careful not to exert too much pressure on the base, where the sensitive detonating cap was placed. But with the other pincers, which were gripping the bullet, he twisted hard, then pulled. The bullet came free from the case. Catsfoot tossed it aside. Then, out of the opened cartridge case he poured the explosive charge of fulminate of mercury. He repeated the process with two other cartridges, until he had a small pile of black powder on a plate. Catsfoot took twelve more shells from the box—the shells with which he was to load his guns. But first, he removed the bullets from each of them and added to them a carefully measured amount of extra powder from the plate. Then he replaced the slugs, making them tight with the pincers.

Finally, he inserted the rounds into his Dragoons.

He now had a pair of guns which were twenty-five per cent over-loaded. When fired, the extra charges would place a great strain on breech and hammer. But there would be no particular danger if the extra-powerful cartridges were not used too often.

Catsfoot was dropping the guns into their holsters when Lucas and Abe came up the ladder. They looked tired and dispirited.

" We talked till we're hoarse," Lucas said, " but we can't get the folks to organise any kind of resistance to Janamo. Some of them agree that'd be a good idea—but they all want to leave it to the others! "

" Do they know what's likely to happen to them?" Catsfoot asked, putting on his fedora. " If I win this fight, it's just possible that the rest of that gang will get away quick, because they'll be scared stiff after losing their leader. But if I lose, they'll turn this town into a hell! What happened last time will be tame by comparison! "

" We know," Abe said. " We tried to tell 'em. But they won't listen. They hope that if they hide from Janamo and keep quiet, mebbe trouble will pass 'em by."

" Then they're fools! " Catsfoot said. " No man ever avoided any kind of trouble by running away from it! "

He tightened the buckle of his gun belt, eased the leg-cords, and led the way down the ladder. The wall clock showed twenty minutes to twelve.

They were crossing the printing department when they heard the harsh, grinding sound of wagon wheels, the creaking of wagon wood, the flapping of canvas covers, and the strained snorting of the horses.

Abe raised his eyebrows.

" Wagon train? Don't get so many of 'em here. And we've heard nothin' about one approachin'."

Quickening their pace, they emerged from the office as a train of eight wagons was halting. A few townsfolk, who had not yet retired to their homes for safety, drifted towards the unexpected arrivals.

A bearded old-timer got off the lead wagon and stumped towards Catsfoot, Lucas and Abe. He was being followed by men, women and children from the wagons.

"Has Janamo visited you yet?" the veteran asked.

Catsfoot only partly hid his surprise.

"Not yet—but he's coming in at high noon. He wants too meet me—and the feeling's mutual."

"Would you be Catsfoot?"

"I am. How do . . .?"

"Don't talk yet!" The wagon master rapped. "There's only time for me to talk! After the gunfight, that gang's goin' to burn down the whole of this town. We heard that big gorilla say so hisself, and he ain't the sort man to make jokes!"

"Burn the town!" Lucas repeated. "You sure that's right? How d'you know?"

The wagon master told them the story, from the time they welcomed Janamo's men, thinking they were U.S. Cavalry.

He finished by bellowing: "We've taken more'n enough from that band o' Mexies. We're goin' to fight 'em, and we're goin' to do it right here in your burgh! We've had all our guns smashed up, but I figure you'll be able to fit us out with more—just loaned."

Only a moderate number of townsfolk had gathered. But its size was increasing quickly as word spread about the intention to burn down Meditation. Sickened horror showed in every face. . . .

Horror—and the first flicker of fighting fury. . . .

Abe turned to them. He said: "These wagoners *want* to fight—and this ain't their town! They came here special to tell us about the plan to burn us down, and now they're ready to . . ."

A miner interrupted. He shouted: "Who in tarnation's that?"

He was pointing along the main street.

A very fat mare was approaching at a dignified canter. But the man in the saddle was far from being dignified.

Lucas breathed in awed, semi-disbelief: "It's Buddy! Buddy in a horse-blanket!"

They moved in a packed mass towards Buddy. When they reached him he was dismounting awkwardly, while holding the blanket up to his neck. If anyone there had been tempted to laugh, they were discouraged by Buddy's face. No one had ever seen Buddy look like this before. The crafty cunning seemed to have gone. In its place there was a form of simmering fury, controlled yet deadly, which could be felt like heat from a fire.

There was a dramatic change in his voice too, as he said: "Wait here for just a couple of minutes, folks, and I'll be with you. I know we don't have much time—but give me two minutes!"

The horse-blanket laced round him, he ran into his saloon.

Abe said to Catsfoot: "We've got the wagoners rarin' to fight, so let's get 'em organised. It needs only about ten minutes to high noon!"

"We'll give Buddy his two minutes," Catsfoot said. "I've a hunch it might be worth it."

Now, suddenly, the main street was becoming packed with people. It seemed that every man, woman and child in Meditation was there. They were chattering in eager, excited groups.

A man in rough canvas trousers, a rancher's blue shirt, and with a superbly efficient Spencer repeating carbine held under his arm, came clattering across the boardwalk from the saloon. A man whose eyes had a glitter which was deadly dangerous.

"I'm ready," the man said, stopping in front of Catsfoot. "Let's get ready for 'em!"

It was Buddy Lane.

Catsfoot put a hand on Buddy's shoulder and squeezed it.

"Good to have you with us," he said.

"We can blast 'em as soon as they ride into town! We can take 'em on both sides and they won't have a chance!"

Catsfoot shook his head.

"Can't be done that way, Buddy. First, I've got to meet

Janamo. Whatever happens to me, you can all start fighting if they try to burn down the town—or if they won't get out of town. But I've got to make my play with Janamo first."

"Why run the risk, Catsfoot? We can nail Janamo easy, now we're all ready to fight!"

"Mebbe we could—but if we did, we'd be no better than him and his mob," Catsfoot said. "We'd be plain killers, shooting people who haven't a chance to defend themselves. Then mebbe, over the years, a legend would grow up about Janamo. Folks'd say he was shot in the back, he was one man against a whole town, and he was really a hero. That's the sort of thing that does happen. And what about me? *I* came out here to fight Janamo, remember? I can't duck out now, Buddy!"

Buddy was quiet for a few moments. Then he nodded.

"Okay—but let's get ready for the time we can shoot 'em!"

The next five minutes contained a miracle of improvisation and organisation.

Women, children, and some protesting older men, were cleared off the streets and into their homes.

Rifles and revolvers (some of them in a frightening state of disrepair) were found and distributed. Small rations of ammunition were issued to each man.

Then, in grim-faced groups, they took up concealed positions in and behind buildings.

The eight covered wagons, with their teams of horses, were moved into a side street.

When high noon came, Meditation had the appearance of a terrified town, the boardwalks empty, the stores, the saloons, the eating houses, all deserted. Yet the place was still fully inhabited—any stranger entering for the first time could sense that.

To Janamo and his men, approaching from the south, it seemed that the town which would not fight, had lacked the courage even to run away.

Janamo had taken his stance in the centre of the road, outside Abe's mercantile store.

Catsfoot faced him, thirty paces away.

There was company for Catsfoot. It was the stray dog which usually prowled about Abe's store. Illogically, Catsfoot felt glad that it was sitting directly in front of him and facing him. Because it was there, he did not feel quite so alone.

Janamo's men had dismounted and were gathering on the boardwalk fronting Abe's store. Mostly, they appeared in-indifferent. They had seen Janamo in this sort of set gunfight often enough.

Catsfoot tilted his wide-brimmed fedora slightly forward. Shrivelling heat from the sun was causing a glare as it bounced back from the baked earth.

Janamo bent to check his leg-cord. While he was doing that, Catsfoot flexed his fingers and eased his elbow muscles several times.

Janamo straightened and at once became hideously massive. He was in no hurry. He spent quite a time dapping his sweating face with a neckcloth. Then, raising his voice only a little, Janamo called: " Okay, Catsfoot, I'm ready to take you . . . I'm comin' in. . . ."

His right hand held flat open and just above his gun butt, Janamo began a slow and careful walk towards Catsfoot. He was crouching slightly forward, running his tongue over his moist lips. He was the hunting animal again—concentrating and savouring the imminent moment of the kill.

As Catsfoot walked forward, he kept the same pace as Janamo. But he was standing entirely upright. His arms were hanging at his sides, the fingertips just about level with the bottom of his holsters. And the stray dog walked with him, tongue out and panting, keeping a yard in front.

Again, Catsfoot tasted raw fear. Till now, he had never seen Janamo. This first sight of the man chilled the bone marrow, shrunk the heart. The monster looked capable of absorbing half a dozen bullets comfortably, and without any serious injury, in the vastness of his body.

Janamo gave an impression of being incredibly fast and accurate with that Remington of his, too. You could always sense when a man was an expert with a gun. Catsfoot sensed that this Mexican's gunplay would have the stamp of satanic genius.

The distance between them had closed to ten paces. Easy shooting range. But neither showed sign of making his play.

Janamo began to circle, moving to his right. Catsfoot moved the same way. Now Janamo was bent almost double. Catsfoot remained upright. The dog, suddenly afraid, had vanished.

They had circled twice when Janamo said: "What's y'score, Catsfoot? I'm talkin' about men you're certain you've nailed. Y'score for sure?"

"Don't know. Don't want to know. Never counted."

"Mine's sixty-three. Figure it'll be sixty-four inside a minute."

Catsfoot did not answer. The only sound was their deep, almost painful breathing as they moved three more complete circles.

Suddenly a look of surprise hit Janamo's face. As if he had suddenly seen something on the boardwalk which changed and made unnecessary all that was happening. Surprise was at once followed by a broad, friendly smile.

And at the same time, Janamo shouted: "*Wait, Catsfoot, wait. . . .*"

At the same moment, Janamo's Remington leapt into his hand. The hammer flipped back and lashed down on the rimfire cartridge.

Meditation rocked to the cruel crash of exploding powder.

The stray dog whined and in some distant house a small child began to cry.

A smoke haze rose and began to drift across the street.

Both men were standing. Both were holding their guns. And both were as motionless as figures chiselled from stone.

They remained that way for several weird seconds.

Then a gun hit the ground. The massive body of Janamo followed it, clutching in baffled astonishment at the two closely-grouped .44 holes in his chest. He fell on his back and he died staring at Catsfoot, the baffled and astonished expression still on his face.

But Catsfoot had not finished. Guns still in his hands, he swung round to face the boardwalk where Janamo's men were standing. But he was not needed. The work was being done for him.

There was a rush of many feet, coming from buildings all over the central part of Meditation. Men holding pistols and rifles were appearing and rushing at the Mexicans from all sides. Buddy Lane, with his carbine, was at the front of one attack.

Remaining on the boardwalk, the Mexicans formed into a hollow square, raising their Remingtons.

If they had been a few seconds quicker, or if the attack had been launched a few seconds later, the Mexican defence fire would have been withering, for they were all superb shots and had the fire-discipline of soldiers.

As it was, a ragged fusillade from the charging men was aimed while the Mexicans were still taking first pressure on their triggers.

Most of the shots missed. But a great many shots were fired and some found targets. Enough to cause immediate chaos in the square and the opening of gaps as men dropped.

Then the men of Meditation, along with the men from the wagon train, were among them. For a full minute the hand-to-hand fighting held the bestial terror of the jungle.

Then the few survivors of Janamo's men were glad to put up their hands.

The whole town had helped to re-equip the wagon train and, late in the afternoon, it had gone on its way to El Paso.

At sundown, Catsfoot entered Buddy Lane's saloon to say good-bye to its owner. He found almost the whole of Meditation there.

Abe said: "Y'ought to stay with us a time, Catsfoot. It ain't right, chasin' off like this."

"I'd like to stay," Catsfoot said, "but I've got to make a report to Tucson, then there's trail work for me to do."

"I suppose it's the marshal at Tucson who'll be most interested to know about the end of Janamo," Lucas said.

Catsfoot shook his head and smiled.

"I can think of someone else in Tucson right now who'll be even more interested!"

"Who?"

"I'm thinking of Will Hambert! I guess you'll have Will back here at his forge before long. Mebbe doing some wrestling, too."

There was a shuffle from the middle of the crowd. Bason Thebes appeared. A pale Bason, but one who had almost recovered. He was holding some folded paper under an arm.

"Buddy asked me along partic'ler," Bason told Catsfoot. "He wanted me to take money on account of the knife wound, but I said no, 'cause it wouldn't be right to take money from a new friend!"

There was a slight laugh, but Bason looked serious.

"I've been in many knife-fights," he announced, his voice beginning to boom with authority. "There was a time when I was challenged to a duel to the death with a . . ."

A crash of good-humoured mock applause drowned Bason's story.

When it died away, Lucas said to him: "Why don't you give Catsfoot his farewell present?"

Bason unfolded the paper which had been under his arm. He handed it to Catsfoot.

It was a rush edition of the *Meditation Gazette*.

And a big headline on the front page said:

CATSFOOT OUTGUNS JANAMO
— SAVES THE TOWN